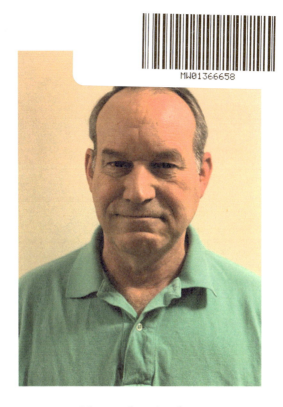

About the Author

I have been a writer my whole life. When I went to college, I fell in love with literature, and I began writing poetry and novels right away. Later in my thirties, I began to paint.

A Stream in the Wild

Paul Devito

A Stream in the Wild

Olympia Publishers
London

www.olympiapublishers.com
OLYMPIA PAPERBACK EDITION

Copyright © Paul Devito 2024

The right of Paul Devito to be identified as author of
this work has been asserted in accordance with sections 77 and 78 of
the Copyright, Designs and Patents Act 1988.

All Rights Reserved

No reproduction, copy or transmission of this publication
may be made without written permission.
No paragraph of this publication may be reproduced,
copied or transmitted save with the written permission of the publisher,
or in accordance with the provisions
of the Copyright Act 1956 (as amended).

Any person who commits any unauthorized act in relation to
this publication may be liable to criminal
prosecution and civil claims for damage.

A CIP catalogue record for this title is
available from the British Library.

ISBN: 978-1-80439-430-4

This is a work of fiction.
Names, characters, places and incidents originate from the writer's
imagination. Any resemblance to actual persons, living or dead, is
purely coincidental.

First Published in 2024

Olympia Publishers
Tallis House
2 Tallis Street
London
EC4Y 0AB

Printed in Great Britain

Dedication

I dedicate this book to my brothers and their families.

Chapter 1

We were walking on a path in the foothills of the Adirondacks, loaded with gear and wearing running shoes. The sun was setting. A deep orange and purple glow hovered above the horizon. The birds were in the trees chirping and singing, while the brush in the wild surrounding us was alive with animals. The path had rocks on it, some large, some small, making it quite difficult to hike. At one point, I heard a waterfall not far from us. We got off the path and struggled through the brush to find the stream. After a few hundred feet, we came upon this beautiful waterfall in the middle of the forest. There were wildflowers on the edge of the falls, and moss was growing on the rocks.

Nancy and I watched intently as the water cascaded over the rocks. It was as if the drops of water were being interrupted on their journey by outside influences. Nancy was my wife of three years, and we were in our mid-thirties. We had set up camp down below this small mountain, and we decided to follow the stream down to our camp. I noticed there were fish in the stream, some close to the surface, others further below. The water flowed smoothly in some parts and struggled over rocks in others. Every once in a while, the stream would gather in pools, and the water would move gently in circles, over and under branches that had fallen in.

"I'm hungry," Nancy said. "What time is it?"

"It's almost two. Let's eat our sandwiches," I said.

"Do you want to continue the discussion we were having yesterday?" she said.

"Not really, but if you insist," I said.

"I think this is the perfect time to have a baby," she said.

"But we're not settled financially," I said. "We have some money, but now our paintings aren't selling. We're in a recession," I said.

"My clock is ticking," she said. "Pretty soon, I won't be able to have children," she said.

"I know. But can't we wait a year or two?" I asked.

"A year or two?"

"You'll still be young enough then," I said.

"I don't want to wait that long," she said.

We walked along the stream, but the overgrowth was intense at times. I almost twisted my ankle at one point, and wished I had worn hiking boots. The woods were thick, but we decided to walk a short distance from the stream because it was easier.

"I'm getting tired," she said.

"We'll rest here," I said.

"Guy and Lisa already have a child, and they're working on their second," she said.

"I know. You're always talking about it," I said.

"Our parents will give us money if we need it," she said.

"I'm already getting a considerable amount from my mother. I can't ask her to give us any more," I said.

"Well, my mother wants me to get pregnant so she can play with her grandchildren," she said.

"She already has two," I said.

"Come on, Paul, let's get pregnant," she pleaded.

"All right, all right," I said. "We'll start tonight."

"Oh, I love you so much," she said.

"I love you too," I said.

We finally arrived at camp and discovered that another couple had taken the lean-to next to ours. We were glad to have company and were quick to introduce ourselves.

"Hi, I'm Paul, and this is Nancy. We've been here two days," I said.

"My name is Rich, and this is Jennifer," he said.

Jennifer was absolutely gorgeous, and I saw Nancy give her a jealous look. I couldn't help but feel slightly intimidated by Jennifer's beauty, but that wasn't going to stop me from flirting with her.

"Are you experienced campers? We can help you with whatever you need," I said.

"We go camping all the time," Jennifer said.

"Do you want to eat together tonight? It's always easier to cook as a group," I said.

"Sure. That would be great," Rich said.

"I'm going to fish for a bit. Do you like fish?" I said.

"Fantastic!" Jennifer said.

I got my pole and my boots and went fishing in the nearby stream. I had fly-fishing gear and was going for trout. I couldn't see the fish, as the rocks prevented me from seeing them, but I knew they were there. I stood in the water, near the shore, and cast out into the middle of the stream. After a while, I caught my first trout. I caught several more over the next few hours and had plenty for dinner. I was so excited, running home with a bucket of fish.

"Look, honey," I said to Nancy.

"You did very well, sweetheart. I suppose I have to clean them," she said.

"We'll do it together," I said.

Richard and Jennifer came over to see my catch.

"You're a wonderful fisherman," Jennifer said.

"Not bad, old man," Rich said.

"Nobody fishes these streams, so there's plenty of fish," I said.

"I used to fish as a kid, but I haven't done it in a long time," Rich said.

"Will you take me fishing?" Jennifer said.

"Sure," I said. "Tomorrow."

Nancy and I spent half an hour cleaning the fish and talking about having our first child.

"If it's a boy, we'll name him Marco, after your brother," she said.

"What if she's a girl?" I said.

"Laura," she said, "or Lynda."

"Those are nice names. I dated a Laura in college," I said.

"You never told me about her," Nancy said.

"We didn't go out for very long. She didn't like the fact that I smoked pot," I said.

"But you quit after your freshman year, I thought," she said.

"By then it was already over," I said. "She was a good lay though."

"You used to think that about me, too," she said.

"I still do," I said.

"Then how come we don't do it nearly as often as we used

12

to?" she said.

"Every couple is like that," I said. "The first year, you make love all the time. Then the physical passion fades, but you're still good in bed."

"Well, now that I'm trying to get pregnant, we'll have to do it more often," she said.

"That's all right with me," I said.

After cleaning the fish, I relaxed by the stream, while Nancy built a fire. The water moved slowly where we were, and there was a pool where I was sitting. I thought about having a baby with some trepidation; I didn't know it was going to affect my lifestyle. I had quite a bit of freedom, and painted on a regular basis. Nancy was a good painter too, and I hoped we would still have a lot of time to work. When I returned to camp, the fire was roaring, and Nancy was cleaning the pots and pans. Jennifer came over, wearing some tight shorts, and a T-shirt. I tried not to stare at her legs, but it was hard. Nancy was very friendly with her.

"What kind of work do you do?" Nancy said to Jennifer.

"I'm in real estate, but my true passion is the piano," Jennifer said.

"There's no instrument like the piano," I said, "except Miles Davis' trumpet."

"How long have you two been together?" Nancy asked.

"We've only been dating for three months," Jennifer said, "but I think we're in love."

"That's great! We've been married for three years, and dated for two before that. We're planning on having a baby," Nancy said.

I knocked some of the logs down on the fire. It was still

fairly warm out. A few minutes later, Rich came over.

"Hey, what's going on?" he said.

"Getting ready to cook soon," Nancy said.

"We have some canned corn, if you like," Jennifer said.

"That would be great," I said.

Jennifer went to get the corn, and Rich sat down with a beer. The store was only a mile and a half away, so they figured they could carry in some heavy things.

"Do you guys want a beer?" Rich said.

"No. We quit drinking a few years ago," I said.

"We're going to get pregnant anyway," Nancy said.

"Congratulations! First one?" he said.

"Yes, and I hope it's a boy," Nancy said.

"Why?" Rich said.

"I want him to turn out just like Paul," she said.

"Isn't that sweet," I said.

Jennifer came back with two cans of corn, so we decided to start cooking. I put the grate on top of the fire and put butter in the pan. A few minutes later, the fish were ready.

"This is the best meal one could have," I said. "I think I'm going to write something about this trip."

"Do you write?" Rich said.

"A little," I said.

"Jennifer plays a mean piano," he said.

"Yes. She was telling us. Do you have any artistic interests?" Nancy asked.

"I can't draw a stick figure, but I love all the arts. I'm a big jazz fan," he said.

"Me too," I said. "I should have lived in the fifties."

"Who do you like in music?" Nancy asked Jennifer.

"I like Art Tatum, Monk, Miles Davis, Keith Jarrett, all the great jazz masters really," she said. "That's the main thing that attracted me to Richard."

We finished eating, and I walked down to the stream to get some water for the dishes. In the evening light, the slow stream reflected oranges and greens against the forest and sky backdrops. Nature was at peace, and so was I. I got a bucket of water and brought it back to camp.

"It's getting cooler out. This fire feels good," Nancy said. "How long are you guys staying?"

"We'll probably leave the day after tomorrow. We've got some deals brewing," Jennifer said.

"Maybe we can hike together tomorrow," I said.

"That would be great," Rich said.

We chatted for a while around the fire, and I couldn't help thinking how nice it would be to fuck Jennifer. I was perfectly happy with Nancy, but Jennifer was so hot, I couldn't stop thinking about her sexually.

"I'm going to go read in the lean-to," Nancy said. "I have this novel by Jane Austen."

"I'm going to bed," Rich said.

Jennifer and I sat by the fire and talked. It was getting considerably cooler out, so we got close to the fire and sat closely together. She had put jeans on, and they clung tightly against her body.

"Did you think of pursuing the piano originally?" I asked.

"I thought about it, but I wasn't good enough. Actually, when I was about twenty, I really was pretty good, but I decided I didn't want to be poor the rest of my life," she said.

"Do you still play regularly?" I said.

"Not as much anymore, but I'm thinking I might get into it again if I can stabilize my finances," she said. "How do you pull it off? It must be impossible to sell your paintings."

"I live off of a trust fund. I'm lucky. We have money in the family," I said.

"That's fantastic! I wish I had that," she said.

"I sell a few paintings now and then and so does Nancy, but we could never support ourselves on that," I said.

"What kind of work do you do?" she said.

"It's impressionistic with a modern flavor," I said. "I do masks and figures in a primitive way. There are some landscapes and seascapes."

"Sounds interesting! You'll have to show them to me some time," she said.

"You don't live too far from us. We'll have to stay in touch," I said.

"I'd love to hear you play the piano."

"You and Nancy can come over for dinner sometime, and I'll play," she said.

I wasn't looking for that response. I would have preferred to see her alone, but I could wait. I didn't really think that I would have an affair, but my fantasies were going strong.

"How old are you, Jennifer?" I said.

"Twenty-eight."

"You're very mature for your age," I said.

"Thank you. I think you're mature, too," she said.

"I've been through a lot. That's probably why I'm more mature than most males my age," I said.

"Care to share?" she said.

"Well, I had a nervous breakdown when I was about your

16

age. I was working too hard on a philosophy paper. I stayed up for several nights and finally went off the deep end," I said. "Fortunately, I recovered completely."

"I'm sorry to hear that," she said.

"I also had a problem with pot," I said, "but I conquered that as well."

"You seem to be perfectly normal," she said. "I've had some problems too, like everybody."

"Like what?"

"I lost my mother when I was fourteen, and I've been in therapy ever since," she said. "My father didn't take it well and was fairly abusive."

"That's too bad, but you seem perfectly normal too," I said.

"I've adjusted," she said.

"You're incredibly beautiful," I said.

"I don't take compliments well either," she said with a laugh.

"At least you have a sense of humor. Most people don't," I said.

"That's one thing I don't like about Rich. He doesn't make me laugh much," she said.

"I think that's a main ingredient. Nancy and I make each other laugh," I said.

"I like Nancy. I think you did very well," she said.

The fire was burning down, so I threw a few logs on it. I could hear the stream in the background and thought how well I would sleep that night. I always slept well when camping out in the fresh air and when my body was tired.

"It must be getting time to go to bed," she said. "I know you have a job to do tonight," she said, laughing.

"It's hard work, but somebody's got to do it," I said. "Let's talk a bit more though."

"All right," she said. "What sexual positions do you like?"

"I like doing it from behind," I said.

"I like it that way, too," she said. "I'm a screamer. You might hear us."

"I'm pretty quiet, but I can get Nancy going sometimes," I said.

We both talked for another half hour. Then I went to the lean-to. Nancy was asleep with her book on her chest. I woke her up and turned down the lantern.

"Hi," I said.

"Hi, sweetheart," she said. "Are you in the mood?"

"Sure," I said, thinking about how Jennifer had got me excited.

It was cold out and I had a hard time getting an erection, but finally I did, and fucked Nancy as hard as I could. She made some loud noises, and I thought about Rick and Jennifer listening to us. Afterwards, I lay exhausted on my sleeping bag and talked to Nancy.

"Did you come?" I asked her.

"Yes. That was great," she said.

"If that doesn't make you pregnant, nothing will," I said, laughing.

"This is really not the best time in my cycle. We're going to have to keep trying."

"That's all right with me," I said.

"What if we can't have a child?" she said.

"Why would you even think that way?"

"I don't know. It's possible."

"Don't worry about that now. We're only getting started," I said. "Now let's get some sleep."

I fell right to sleep and slept right through until the morning. I had a sexual dream about having Jennifer and Nancy at the same time, and I laughed to myself when I awakened. I always got up before Nancy, and I went down to the stream to wash with our biodegradable soap. The sun was up, and the birds were chirping away. It was my favorite time of the day. The air was cool, and the water was freezing. I rolled up my jeans and took my shirt off. I joyously stepped into the stream, and my feet froze right away. I splashed some water on myself and washed quickly. A few minutes later, Nancy walked down and said hello.

"I'm pregnant!" She laughed.

"I told you it would work out," I said.

"Are you going to fish this morning?" she asked.

"Definitely," I said.

"I'm going to hike to the store to get some provisions," she said.

"I'll see you later," I said.

I got out of the water and dried off. The sun was up, and it was going to be another beautiful day. I got my fly rod and fished for a while. Jennifer came down to the stream and asked me how the fishing was going.

"I've caught two so far. I think we'll be having fish for breakfast too," I said.

"We've got some eggs," she said.

"That'll be great."

"Turn around. I'm going to take my top off to wash," she said.

"Oh," I said.

I turned around and waited a few seconds. Then I turned back to get a good look at her.

"You're peeking!" she screamed with a laugh.

"I couldn't help myself," I said, looking right at her.

"Turn away!" she said, laughing.

I went back to fishing and said, "I caught a big one this time!"

"You're a bad boy," she said.

"You have no idea," I said.

She finished washing and dried off by the edge of the stream. Her breasts were firm and perfect. Now I lusted after her more than ever. Nancy came back an hour later and brought some bacon and more eggs. There was no fish for breakfast, so we cooked what we had on our small stove. Rick was cheerful that morning and had slept in. Jennifer and I kept our secret to ourselves.

Chapter 2

After breakfast, I fished some more with limited success. I kept the two fish that I had caught, alive in the bucket. We all decided to go hiking later that morning, and I brought my camera with me. Nancy and Rich walked ahead, while Jennifer and I walked behind.

"I'm sorry for peeking at you earlier," I said to Jennifer.

"That's all right. I don't care," she said.

"You have a beautiful body," I said.

"Thank you," she said.

"Are you pretty serious about Rich?" I said.

"I think so, but I'm still young; I'd like to live in Italy or France before I settle down."

"I lived in Italy for a year when I was a senior in college," I said. "It was the best year of my life."

"Whereabouts?"

"In Florence."

"I've seen a lot of pictures of Florence. It's a beautiful city," she said.

The climb was getting harder as we approached the summit of the mountain. There were fewer and fewer trees as we ascended, and we could see the top of the mountain, which was bald.

"Have you ever done any modeling?" I asked her.

"A little when I was younger, but I'm really not tall

enough," she said.

"I'd like to paint your portrait," I said.

"Nude?"

"Not necessarily," I replied.

"I'd love that," she said. "Is that what you usually paint?"

"No. My style is more modern. I paint masks, seascapes, wild skies. You'll see them."

"Sounds very interesting," she said.

We finally made it to the summit, and we were so exhausted, we sat down and admired the scenery. The view was intense. There were mountains as far as the eye could see. We had brought sandwiches, and we ate in silence for a few minutes. I was looking at Nancy, her face red from the exercise, but I was thinking about Jennifer in her tight shorts.

"I would love to have a cabin in the mountains," Rich said.

"It would be a great place to paint," Nancy said.

"And fish," I said.

We walked around the top of the mountain as I took pictures. The sky was mostly blue with a few puffy white clouds. We stayed up there about an hour, and then began our descent. I was fairly tired, as were Nancy and Rich, but it was perfectly evident that Jennifer had plenty of energy left. Jennifer and I walked behind again and had fun with each other. It didn't take too long to get to the bottom, and I put on my swimsuit to go in the stream. Nancy and Jennifer went around to look for wood, and Rich relaxed in their lean-to.

The water was freezing, but it felt good on my hot body. I thought about having our first child, and I was scared. I knew nothing about raising a child. I didn't want to stay up all night with a crying baby, and I was committed for the rest of my life.

22

I loved Nancy, but these thoughts about Jennifer scared me. I got out of the water. My skin was turning blue, and I went to dry off. Jennifer and Nancy were sitting and talking.

"We're talking about you," Nancy said.

"Nothing derogatory, I hope," I said.

"No. I was telling her about your poetry," Nancy said.

"She likes my poetry more than my fiction," I said.

"Your poetry is so romantic," Nancy said.

"So is my fiction," I said.

"Well, I'll have to judge for myself," Jennifer said.

"Here comes Rich," I said.

"Hi, guys," he said.

"How was your nap?" Jennifer said.

"Not bad," he said. "Shall we build a fire?"

"Sure," Nancy said.

The four of us built a fire and lit it. We made it with big logs, so that it would be slow burning.

"My brother is named Richard," I said. "He's into real estate, too. He plays the guitar and sings."

"They're very close," Nancy said. "Paul's close to his whole family. My family is more difficult.

"Nancy is the only sane one in her family," I said, "but her father is cool."

"I'm very close to my father," Jennifer said.

"Daddy's little girl," Rich said. "Both my parents died in a car wreck when I was young. I was raised by my aunt and uncle."

"That must have been hard on you," I said.

"I was so young I didn't really know them. My aunt and uncle were like my parents," he said.

23

"Let's eat hot dogs tonight," Nancy said.

"Good idea," Jennifer said.

We got out the hot dogs and bread, and Jennifer had some mustard. We cooked the dogs over the fire, and it felt like a spiritual experience. The fire kept us warm, but our backs were getting colder. It was a beautiful night, and the moon was out. I reflected on my first date with Nancy and how infatuated I had been. That infatuation had worn off, but my love had only strengthened.

"Let's talk about sex," Jennifer said with a laugh.

"What about it?" Rich said.

"I don't know. What was the craziest place you ever made love?" Jennifer said.

"I got a blow job in a restaurant once," Rich said, "but only for a few seconds. My girlfriend and I were in college, and we were pretty drunk. I don't think anybody saw us."

"The only time I didn't do it in a bed was in a car," I said.

"I did it on a beach at night," Nancy said. "What about you, Jennifer?"

"I did it in a phone booth when I was fourteen," she said. "It was my first time, and it was a disaster." She laughed.

"That's a good story," I said.

We finished eating and cleaned up. I put some more logs on the fire and we sat around chatting for a long time. Nancy and I went to bed early and left the other two sitting by the fire. We made love in the double sleeping bag, and I came inside her for the second day in a row.

"I love you so much," she said afterwards.

"I love you too," I said.

We slept pretty well that night, but I got up very early. I

decided to let Nancy sleep, and I went out to go fishing. The sun was barely up, and it looked like it was going to be another perfect day. I caught two trout and pulled them out with alacrity. I felt so peaceful when I fished. I would watch the water move downstream with sparkles, and everything else was at rest. When I finished fishing, I went back up to camp and built a fire. I cleaned the fish and felt happy. Some of the initial fear of having a child had subsided. I saw Jennifer up and moving around and called to her.

"Hey, what's up," I said.

"Cleaning up a bit. That's all," she said.

She came over and sat next to me by the fire.

"We're leaving tomorrow," I said.

"So are we," she said. "We have to get back to work."

"I want to see you when we get back to town," I said.

"You will," she said, "and I might pose nude." She laughed.

"I was thinking of something more exotic, like leather underwear," I said.

"With chains?" she said.

"Sure, why not?" I said.

Nancy came out of the lean-to and sat by the fire.

"It's chilly this morning," she said.

"Some of the leaves are starting to turn," Jennifer said.

"The birds are so loud out here," Nancy said. "I can never sleep in the morning."

"Why don't you jump in the stream? That'll wake you up," I said to Nancy.

"No, thank you," she said. "I'd rather stink," she said, laughing.

25

"I caught two fish," I said, "and I cleaned them."

"Let's have breakfast then. I'll get Rich up," Jennifer said.

Nancy and I began cooking the fish, and we added some eggs and bacon. I didn't feel like hiking that day. All I wanted to do was read and fish. Jennifer and Rich came over, and we ate. The food tasted delicious, and I wished we could stay a few more days, but we had commitments.

"What are you guys doing today?" I said to Rich and Jennifer.

"We're going to take photographs of birds," Jennifer said. "There are supposed to be some hawks around here."

"We saw a few the other day," Nancy said, "up the mountain a little ways."

After eating, we cleaned up, and I took a bath in the stream. I couldn't stop thinking about fucking Jennifer. It had been a long time since I had fucked anyone else. I had never cheated on Nancy. Rich and Jennifer took off, and Nancy decided to read for a while. I went fishing and had a long dry spell. The fish were easier to catch early in the morning. I had some of my best ideas while I was fishing. It relaxed me and made it easier to concentrate. After fishing for a few hours, I decided to take another dip in the stream. I took all my clothes off and went into a pool that was not too far from camp. The water was refreshing, and it woke me right up. Nancy was still reading when I got back, and she had put a pot of coffee on our stove. I had some coffee and talked to Nancy for a while.

"Do you want to have sex this afternoon?" Nancy asked.

"I hate planning it out this way," I said.

"Well, we have to plan; we have to have sex as often as possible for a while," she said.

26

"Not this afternoon. Tonight will be better," I said.

"Do you still enjoy having sex with me?" she asked.

"Of course I do," I said.

"Then why don't you want to have it this afternoon?" she said.

"I'm not in the mood. That's all. Let's not have this conversation again," I said.

"Don't be angry. I'm just insecure," she said.

"You should be perfectly confident," I said.

"I know you love me. It's the sex thing I'm not so confident about. I notice how you look at Jennifer," she said.

"Jennifer?" What's she got to do with this?" I said.

"Admit it. You'd love to fuck her," she said.

"I've had enough. I'm going fishing," I said.

I left in a huff and took my gear down to the stream. I could see Nancy going back to her book by the fireplace. I wasn't angry, but I had a feeling of guilt or of being found out. I fished for two hours or so and only caught one fish. I walked back to camp in better spirits and sat next to Nancy.

"Let's have sex," I said.

"Do you mean it?" she said.

"Come on, before they get back," I said.

We went into the lean-to, and I fucked her hard, out of a feeling of guilt. She talked dirty to me, which I really liked, and it was one of the best fucks we had ever had. Not much later, Rich and Jennifer got back to camp. They were exhausted, but they said they had had a great time.

"We took some wonderful pictures, and we did find some hawks," Jennifer said.

"I think we're having hot dogs for dinner again, unless you

guys can come up with something else," Nancy said.

"We have some baked beans and corn," Jennifer said.

We built a fire and cooked our food. It was cool again that evening, but the moon came out, and we all felt at peace. I tried to forget what Nancy had said earlier, but it echoed in my mind once in a while. The food tasted so good out in the fresh air, though it was only hot dogs and beans.

"Rich and I are leaving early in the morning," Jennifer said.

"We'll have to get together soon, once we get back into town," I said.

"We can't wait to see your art work," Jennifer said.

"We can't wait to hear you play the piano," Nancy said.

After eating, Rich and I cleaned up, while the women went to look for more wood.

"Are you pretty serious about Jennifer?" I asked Rich.

"Yes, I'm serious," he said. "I've never had a relationship that was so positive before."

"Positive in what way?"

"She's always building me up. She makes me feel good about myself. She never tears me down. I'm not used to that. The women I've gone out with were always pointing out my flaws, only to make themselves feel superior. This is different."

"Sounds great," I said. "Nancy's positive with me, too, most of the time. We respect each other. I think that's important."

"That's vital, and trust too," he said.

After cleaning up, we decided to take a dip in the stream. We put on our bathing suits and went to the pool I had been to before. The water was freezing as usual, but the sun was going down, so it was even colder. We didn't care. We were only going in for a few seconds to get refreshed. The water swirled around the pool as I reflected on my conversation with Richard. I noticed myself feeling jealous of Jennifer, and I quickly pushed that feeling away.

"You go first," I said.

Rich jumped in and came up screaming with delight.

"Ohh, that's cold," he yelled.

I jumped in after he came out and said calmly, "Oh, it's not so bad."

We grabbed our towels and put on our t-shirts. Then we ran back to the fire where the women were sitting.

"You guys are crazy," Nancy said.

"I can't wait to get back home to my hot bathtub," Rich said.

"You'll probably use cold water anyway," Jennifer said.

Rich and I went to get dressed, while the women built up the fire. I put four layers of clothes on and sat between my wife and Jennifer. Rich came out with a heavy coat, and we all laughed.

"I don't know why he brought that coat," Jennifer said. "He's too skinny."

"Just for such occasions," Rich said.

It was a beautiful big fire, and I enjoyed watching the sparks float up to the pine trees. We stared at the fire, as if hypnotized, and Rich took off his coat after he got warmed up. I held Nancy's hand, while I stared at Jennifer's legs.

"The first thing I'm going to do when I get home tomorrow is take a hot shower," Jennifer said.

"Me too," Nancy said.

"We should camp together in the spring," Rich said.

"We're up for that," I said, "but not when the bugs are bad."

"Have you ever camped in the winter?" Jennifer asked.

"No way," I said.

"I did once," she said. "I only lasted a day and a half. It's too hard."

"I want to enjoy the beautiful summer days and nights when I go camping," Nancy said.

"It's too hard to have sex when you go camping in the winter," I said.

"We don't believe in sex," Jennifer said, laughing.

"We only do it when we're trying to get pregnant," Nancy said.

"And on holidays," I said.

We laughed and talked for quite a while, until Nancy gave me the signal that it was time for bed. We said good night and went to our cabin. We could hear the others talking as we took our clothes off in the sleeping bag.

"I love you so much," Nancy said.

"I love you too," I said.

We made love in the dark, which I didn't like, and were perfectly silent. I moved slowly for a long time, trying to make Nancy come, but it didn't work, so I sped up and came inside her.

"That felt good," she whispered.

"Yeah, it was great," I said.

We went to sleep, and I slept for a few hours, until I heard a noise outside the lean-to. I got the flashlight and went outside. There, in our food, was a raccoon. I threw a stick at him and he scampered off. I went back to bed and slept until the morning.

Nancy always slept better than I did, and she slept until eight o'clock. I was up at six and decided to do some fishing before picking up for our trip home. The sun wasn't even up yet, but the sky was a light blue. I put on my gear and walked down to the stream. The birds were singing, and the stream was making its rushing noise.

I walked out carefully, steadying myself on individual rocks. I cast out with my fly rod and almost immediately caught a fish. I was elated and cast out some more, catching a total of five fish. The fish weren't that large, but it was the principle of the thing. I took them back to camp and cleaned them. It was still cool, as the sun had just risen, and I built a fire. After a while, Jennifer came over in her tight jeans and sat down.

"How was your night?" she asked.

"Pretty good. There was a raccoon here. I chased him off," I said.

"I didn't sleep very well," she said.

"What's the matter?"

"I'm worried about money," she said.

"I didn't realize you were having problems," I said.

"I haven't made a sale in two months. The market has been terrible," she said.

"Do you want me to loan you some money?" I said.

"Oh, I couldn't do that," she said, "but that's very kind of you."

"No, please, let me help you. I have extra money that I could loan you. I trust you. I'm sure it would be all right with Nancy."

"I'll think about it," she said.

Then, suddenly, I kissed her on the cheek. It came out of

31

nowhere, but she smiled and blushed.

"I'm sorry. I didn't mean that," I said.

"Of course you meant it, and it's quite all right. I liked it," she said.

I turned around to see if Nancy had been looking, but she was still asleep.

"I really like you, Jennifer," I said.

"I like you too," she said with a smile.

I heard Nancy stirring, so I didn't say another word. I got up and put another two logs on the fire. Nancy came out in her jeans and sweatshirt. She looked pretty good in the mornings, before she put her makeup on, which, of course, she never did when we were camping.

"Look, I caught some fish," I said to Nancy.

"I see that. Good for you," she said. "I'll cook them. Good morning, Jennifer."

"Good morning, Nancy," she said.

Nancy cooked the fish and added a few eggs. We ate with gusto. The food was so good.

"We have to get moving pretty soon," Nancy said.

"It won't take me long to pack," I said.

"We're going to miss you guys," I said to Jennifer.

"We'll see you back in the city," Jennifer said.

Rich got up a short while later, as we were getting ready to leave, so we said goodbye. I wanted to give Jennifer a hug and kiss, but only shook her hand. I took one last look at the stream and was saddened by its beauty. It only took us half an hour to get back to the car, but carrying the backpacks had made us tired. The car started right up, and we were off.

Chapter 3

It was about a two-hour drive back to Syracuse, and it was a beautiful drive. The roads were winding, and the old rustic villages were quaint. I wasn't looking forward to going back to our routine life, but it was somewhat exciting that we were planning on having a baby.

"That was a nice trip," Nancy said.

"It was great, and the fishing was good," I said.

"If it's a boy, we're going to name him after you," Nancy said.

"No, definitely, not," I said, "but maybe after one of my brothers, or my father."

"Okay, but if it's a girl, I want to name her after my grandmother," she said.

"That's fine," I said.

We stopped on the way and got a cup of coffee at a diner. I could smell autumn coming in the air. Nancy and I knew each other so well that we didn't have to talk for long periods of time. We got back in the car and finished the drive home.

We lived in a cute old house in a town called Fayetteville, outside of Syracuse. The town had been around for a long time, and some of the shops and restaurants had old black and white pictures of the village when it had first started out. Most of the houses were Victorian, painted in various colors. The town had a lot of charm, and we enjoyed living there.

I brought some of the feeling of the stream back with me. I could see in my imagination the water rushing over the rocks and the reflective pools swirling around in circles. The feelings of the outdoors changed in the city, but like my camping days as a child, they stayed with me. When we got home, we unpacked the car and went to bed. I was tired from not getting enough sleep on the trip, and my body was sore. Nancy was tired too, so we slipped into bed and took a two-hour nap.

"What time is it?" Nancy asked, after our nap.

"A few days in the woods without a clock, and now we have to keep track of time," I said. "It's almost three."

"I have to call my mother," she said.

"So do I," I said.

Nancy called her mother and talked to her for almost an hour. They mostly talked about the new baby, and her mother was excited to be a grandmother. Afterwards, I called my mother and talked to her for half an hour.

"What did she say?" Nancy asked.

"She said she was glad that we are planning on a baby, and not to think that it was going to be easy. She wants to make sure that I share the responsibility. We talked about Dad for a while, and she said he was busy with his investments and real estate holdings. Of course, she doesn't talk to him much, but that's what she said," I answered.

"Okay, well, I have to go to the store and get some groceries," she said.

"Do you want me to go with you?" I said.

"No. I'll go," she said.

After she left, I had an impulse to call Jennifer, but I figured I would wait a few days. I called my best friend Greg

34

instead.

"Hey, what's up?" he said.

"Hey, stranger, I missed you," I said.

"How was your trip?" he said.

"Better than I ever expected," I said.

"What happened?" he said.

"There was this other couple camping next to us, and she was hot. I got to see her naked as she was bathing in the stream," I said.

"Did Nancy know?" he said.

"No. She was off doing something else," I said, "and I have her phone number here in town."

"You're not thinking of doing anything, are you?" he said.

"Well, I'm thinking about it. I'm telling you, she's hot," I said.

"Don't think about it. You and Nancy have something very special. I've seen too many people throw it away," he said.

"Mostly I'm only fantasizing, but I must admit, I can't stop thinking about her. By the way, Nancy and I are planning on having a baby," I said.

"Even more reason to behave yourself," he said.

"I know, I know, but I can't imagine going the rest of my life without ever having sex with anyone else," I said.

"That's a commitment you made," he said. "You're only going to fuck up what you already have," he said.

"I didn't expect so much moralizing from you," I said.

"What else did you expect? You know I made that same mistake with my first wife," he said.

"Yeah, I guess you're right. Thanks for the advice. I'll talk to you tomorrow," I said.

"Later," he said, and hung up.

It was funny. I felt guilty already, and I hadn't done anything. I wanted to be outdoors fishing or lying flat in the stream, the water rushing over me. I waited for Nancy to come back with some food. I was pretty hungry. She came home an hour later and cooked some hamburgers.

"The sex has been different since we've started trying to have a baby," she said.

"How so?" I said.

"It's more intense," she said.

"In what way?" I said.

"I don't know. You have more style. You start slowly, build up, and then end in a crescendo. It's wonderful!" she said.

"Well, I'm glad you like it," I said.

"I think we should experiment more though, try different positions, and do it more often," she said.

"We can do all that," I said.

"How's that hamburger?" she asked.

"Delicious," I said.

"Let's make love after we eat," she said.

"Can't we do it tonight?" I said.

"You said we could do it more often. Let's do it now and tonight," she said.

"You're insatiable," I said.

"I like the way we've been doing it lately," she said.

We finished eating and went into the bedroom. The bedroom was decorated nicely, but simply. There were beige curtains and an Oriental rug. Candles were placed on the end tables and on the dresser. The furniture was all antique. She started to take her clothes off, as usual, but I stopped her.

We got under the covers with all our clothes on and began kissing. I imagined kissing Jennifer for a second, but then came back to reality. The passion in our kissing had faded, but I made a half-hearted attempt to swirl my tongue around. The first few months of our relationship, I had gone down on her with pleasure, but now it turned me off. I rubbed her back before taking off her blouse. Her tits were still firm, and I put my mouth on her nipples. I took her pants off but left her panties on. I put my hand under the cloth and massaged her clitoris. She moaned as I rubbed it ever so gently. I wasn't excited, even though she put her mouth on my cock. I entered her and moved slowly. I sped up after a while, my cock not too hard. I tried to come, but I couldn't.

"I'm sorry," I said.

"What's the matter?" she said.

"I don't know really. I'm not into it, I guess."

"You were so good on the camping trip," she said.

"You know how much I love being out in nature," I said. "It's not the same here in the city."

"That's bullshit," she said.

"Don't be angry. Sometimes these things happen."

"I know, but don't make up some lame excuse," she said.

"I don't know what's wrong. We'll try again tomorrow. Okay?"

"All right. I'm sorry too," she said.

We got up and showered together. I rubbed soap all over her body. I really did love her. She rubbed soap on my cock, and I got hard. After our shower, Nancy went over to a friend's house, and I read. I enjoyed my time alone. I could always entertain myself. I was reading Thomas Hardy, *Jude the*

Obscure, for the third time. I had studied it in graduate school, and I had fond memories attached to it. I fell asleep after reading for a few hours and awakened when Nancy arrived home.

"Hi," she said.

"Did you have a nice time over at Linda's house?" I asked.

"We talked a lot about babies. Her son is just starting to talk," she said.

"He's talking early," I said.

"I know. He's only ten months old," she said.

"What do you want to have for dinner? I'll cook," I said.

"Maybe a couple of hot dogs," she said, "nothing fancy."

I fixed four hot dogs and made a salad. We often ate simply and lived simply. Now with a possible child, life would become much more complicated. I didn't know if my impotence was related to my fear of having a child or not. I was hardly ever impotent, but it disturbed me nonetheless. I almost always had an orgasm, but I could sense that something was wrong. I thought about Jennifer for a moment and knew I could have an orgasm with her.

"Let's try again later," Nancy said.

"I think I need to take a break for a day," I said.

"Okay, but I know we'll do better tomorrow," she said.

"I hope so," I said.

We cleaned up after dinner and sat down to watch a movie. Very few movies interested me, but I loved the medium. It was a Jane Austen film, and all I could think was how a great novel could translate so poorly to film. We went to bed early, and I slept pretty well. When I got up in the morning, I remembered a dream I had about being in the woods and making love to

Jennifer. I realized I was becoming obsessed with Jennifer, but there seemed to be nothing I could do about it.

"Good morning, sweetheart," I said to Nancy.

"Good morning," she said cheerfully.

I went in the bathroom and brushed my teeth. I usually exercised in the morning, but I decided to skip it. Nancy put her sweats on and went for a walk. I decided to call Jennifer to see how she was doing. At that moment, I didn't have any particular intentions. I only wanted to talk to her.

"Hi. This is Paul," I said.

"Hi. How are you? How was your trip back?" she said.

"It was fine. We took our time and enjoyed the scenery," I said. "I was calling to see how you're doing."

"I'm fine. I didn't sleep that well last night. Rich slept at his place, and I'm kind of getting used to sleeping next to him," she said. "I have a lot of work to do today. I have to get ready to go into the office. Can I call you later?"

"Sure," I said. "Talk to you later."

When I got off the phone, I thought that she had sounded excited to hear from me. At that point, I was getting some pretty serious intentions of visiting her alone. Nancy got back from her walk and said she felt pretty good. I had had three cups of coffee and was feeling good myself but decided I would try to exercise later, so that I would sleep better. I often had trouble sleeping. My mind would race at times.

"Are you going to paint today?" Nancy asked me.

"No. I don't think so. I'm going to go to the drug store and get my photographs developed and printed up," I said. "What about you?"

"I think I'm going to do some painting," she said.

"Have you thought about your subject?" I said.

"I think I want to do a house in a field," she said.

"That sounds nice," I said.

"With a wild sky and a pond," she said.

"Great," I said.

I couldn't get Jennifer off my mind, and I thought about her even while I was talking to Nancy. I almost started to panic. It was getting so obsessive. I went to the drug store and dropped off the film. I wanted to be in the wild forest again with the birds and squirrels. When I returned, Nancy was busy painting. I made myself a sandwich and tried not to think about Jennifer naked in the stream. I wanted to call her again, but I needed an excuse, and I couldn't think of one. I read for a while, until Nancy finished her painting.

"Come look," she said.

I went into the studio and examined her painting.

"It's excellent," I said.

"I like it too," she said. "I'm excited now. Let's make love."

"All right," I said.

We went into the bedroom and took all our clothes off. I was not very excited, and all I could think about was Jennifer. We lay next to each other, and Nancy put her hands on my cock. She massaged it slowly, until I got semi-hard. Then she put her mouth on it. I got hard and got on top of her, with her lying on her stomach. She put her ass in the air, and I inserted myself.

"Talk dirty," I said.

"Fuck me. Fuck me good," she said.

"I'm going to fuck you so hard," I said.

I thought about Jennifer at that moment and started fucking Nancy as hard as I could.

"Oh, that's good, just like that. Keep fucking me," she said.

I came inside her after a few minutes and fell exhausted next to her.

"Did you come?" she said.

"I sure did," I said.

"Good," she said. "This is a good time in my cycle to get pregnant."

"Now I'm going to sleep for a while," I said.

"Me too," she said.

I fell right to sleep and dreamt of the wilderness in the Adirondacks. I was in the stream fucking Jennifer, and my cock was as hard as a rock. I woke up next to Nancy and almost felt guilty for having that dream. When I woke up, I looked at Nancy in her peaceful sleep and thought that I was crazy for wanting to cheat on her.

"Wake up, sweetheart," I said.

"I had the nicest dream," she said.

"What was it about?" I said.

"I dreamt that we were strolling our baby down the street and that everybody we encountered gave us gifts. I remember being so happy."

"That's a great dream," I said. "We're happy already though."

"Are you really happy, Paul?" she asked.

"Of course," I said. "I wouldn't be trying to have a baby with you if I weren't."

"A lot of people have babies without being happy," she said.

"Well, I'm not one of them," I said.

"I'm glad," she said.

Nancy got out of bed and went to take a shower. I waited for a minute, then decided to join her.

"Hi, stranger," she said.

"Were you able to come?" I said.

"Twice," she said.

"Good for you," I said.

"You're a good lover still," she said.

"I'm glad you think so," I said.

We showered together for a long time, rubbing soap on each other's bodies and playing with each other. We still had a lot of the intimacy that first brought us together, but I couldn't stop thinking about Jennifer. Obsessiveness was not usually part of my personality, but in this case, it took over. I imagined I was playing with Jennifer while I moved my hands across Nancy's body. After our shower, I went into the living room to read, while Nancy cleaned a bit. Sometimes, it felt like we had been married for twenty years. We were so comfortable with each other.

"I'm going for a walk," I said, thinking it would give me an opportunity to call Jennifer.

I walked outside, and it was sprinkling a bit. The rain didn't bother me, but I thought Nancy would think that it was strange for me to be walking. I put my phone up to my ear and decided it was too soon to call. I didn't walk very far and returned home. The phone had gotten wet, so I dried it off, and Nancy noticed.

"Who were you calling in the rain?" she said.

"Richard," I said.

"Your brother?" she said. "Why did you have to wait until you got outside?"

"I just had the urge to call him. He's kind of depressed right now, so I thought I'd cheer him up," I said. "I didn't know it was raining."

"Are you going to call him now?" she said.

"Yes."

I called my brother and talked to him for a while as Nancy listened. He had two daughters and was in the middle of making a big real estate deal, which wasn't going well. I purposefully concentrated on his tough deal to make Nancy think that I was really worried about it. Richard was fine, as I was glad to hear, and I hung up feeling relaxed. Nancy didn't say another word about it.

We decided that I would cook dinner, so I cooked some baked chicken with bread crumbs. I wished I was cooking fish out in the wild. We ate in front of the television, and the news was really bad. I tried not to let the state of the world bother me too much, and I concentrated on my art. My paintings were about nature, for the most part, and the beauty of the wilderness.

"What do you want to do tonight?" Nancy said.

"I'm going to read," I said. "I love my book."

"I think I'll watch a movie," she said.

Later that night, Nancy asked me if I wanted to make love again, and I said no.

"I don't have that much energy anymore," I said.

"But we have to get pregnant," she said.

"Be patient. We will get pregnant," I said.

"I like making love to you twice a day," she said.

"Well, forget it for today," I said.

We went to bed late, and I was exhausted. I was so tired that I had trouble falling asleep. Nancy was snoring, but I finally slept. I had another dream about the Adirondacks, but this time I was on the peak of a mountain, looking over the expanse. Jennifer was next to me, and I went from staring at the view, to staring at her ass. Then, suddenly, she took her clothes off and raised her arms in the air. We made love, and then I woke up with a start.

Nancy was still sleeping, so I got up and took a shower. The dream troubled me. I didn't want to be obsessed with Jennifer, but I couldn't help it. Nancy heard me and joined me in the shower. She wanted to make love that morning, but I told her later.

"I'm starting to get a resentment against you," she said, as we got out of the shower.

"Are you serious? Why?" I said.

"Because you don't really want to fuck me anymore. You're always looking at younger women, and I'm tired of it," she said.

"That's not true," I said.

"Yes, it is," she said.

"Have it your way," I said.

I walked out of the bathroom and went into the kitchen to sulk. I knew she was at least partially right, but I didn't want to admit it to her. I felt terrible that she was feeling resentment. I had never expected it. I thought I should make love to her right away, but I really didn't feel like it. She came out to the kitchen, and I could tell she was in a bad mood.

"I'm sorry," she said.

"You don't mean it," I said.

"I could never really have a resentment towards you, but my feelings are hurt," she said.

"I haven't tried to hurt your feelings," I said. "I still love you."

"I know you love me, but I want the passion we used to have," she said.

"I have some passion left," I said.

"Then why are you always looking at younger women?" she said.

"That's normal. All guys look at other women," I said.

"It still doesn't make me feel good. I wish you'd cut it out," she said.

"All right. I will," I said. "Do you want to make love?"

"Yes."

We made love, and it was good. I came inside her, and I made her orgasm. It was not a chore to make love to her, but while I preferred it three times a week, she wanted it every day.

"That felt really good," she said. "Thank you."

"You don't have to thank me," I said.

"I wanted to," she said.

"Well, it was good for me, too," I said.

We took another quick shower. Then I went out for a walk with my telephone. I knew exactly what I was going to do. I called Jennifer on her cell phone, knowing that she was working.

"What's up?" she said, cheerfully.

"I was wondering if we could have lunch. I have a problem I want to discuss with you," I said.

"Sure. I'll meet you at the Chinese restaurant in the village," she said. "About one?"

"Great," I said.

My heart was beating like crazy, and I had to think of an excuse to get away. When I got back to the house, I had to pretend that I wasn't excited, so I went right to our bedroom. Nancy was watering the plants and didn't even notice my coming in. I sat on the bed and tried to calm down. I decided to tell Nancy that I was having lunch with my friend Greg and hoped that he would cover for me. I called Greg and figured I might as well tell him the truth.

"Hey," he said.

"I need a favor," I said.

"Anything you need," he said.

"I'm having lunch with Jennifer, and I need you to cover for me. I'm going to tell Nancy that I'm having lunch with you. Is that all right?" I said.

"I'm not crazy about the idea, but I owe you a favor anyway," he said. "I'll do it."

"Thanks. I'll talk to you later," I said.

Now I could hardly contain myself. I wondered what Jennifer was thinking about all this. After all, I had only invited her out for lunch. She must have had a suspicion that something was up. I told Nancy I was going out for lunch later and sat down to read. I noticed, after reading a page, that I hadn't comprehended a word. I decided to paint for a while, but that turned into a disaster. I threw the canvas out before Nancy could see it. I didn't know what to do with myself.

"You seem agitated," Nancy said.

"I don't know what's wrong with me today. I'm restless," I said.

"Why don't you take a hot bath? Maybe that'll calm you

down," she said.

"Good idea," I said.

I took a bath and imagined Jennifer in the water with me. I flashed back to the moment I saw her naked in the stream. She had the most perfect breasts and a perfect ass. I thought about what I would say to her at lunch, but nothing sounded right. I wanted to tell her that I wanted to have an affair with her, but I was scared. I knew I should take it slow, but I lusted so much. Besides the sex, I also liked her a lot, which was dangerous. After my bath, I got dressed for lunch. I didn't want to dress up, for fear that Nancy would be suspicious. I put on a pair of jeans and wore a nice striped shirt. I watched television, while Nancy painted, and then it was time to meet Jennifer.

"I'll see you in a while," I said to Nancy.

"Maybe Greg will calm you down," she said.

"I'm sure he will," I said.

I got in the car and checked myself in the mirror. I was as ready as I was ever going to be. I was nervous and tried to calm down by listening to some jazz. When I got to the restaurant, the parking lot was almost empty. I didn't know what kind of a car she was driving, so I figured I had got there before her. I sat down and ordered a pot of tea. She came in a few minutes later and greeted me with a big smile.

"Hi!" she said.

"Hi, yourself!" I said. "Want some tea?"

"Sure."

"I miss the wilderness," I said. "The city is so unexciting compared to the mountains."

"I know what you mean. We had a lot of fun, didn't we?" she said.

"Yes. I'm glad we got to see a lot of each other," I said with a laugh.

"You peeked!" She laughed.

"I really didn't mean to," I said. "It was an accident."

"Sure." She laughed. "How's Nancy?"

"She's mad at me," I said.

"Why?"

"Because she says I lust after other women," I said.

"All men do that," she said.

"That's what I told her," I said. "She feels the passion has faded from our relationship."

"Has it?" she asked.

"I guess it has a little. I mean, I want to have children with her, but the sex isn't great anymore," I said.

"Is that why you're having lunch with me?" she said.

I was taken aback at such a blunt question. I didn't know how to respond.

"Well, I want to be friends with you. I don't know about having sex," I said.

"I think you want to have sex with me," she said. "I want to have sex with you."

"You do?" I said incredulously.

"Yes, I do. I was attracted to you the minute I laid eyes on you," she said.

"I can't believe you're saying all this," I said.

"Isn't this what you want me to say?" she said.

"Yes it is, to be perfectly honest. I'm not going to pretend that I'm not interested," I said.

"Then let's get together sometime, at my place," she said.

"I like your confidence," I said.

"I like your shyness," she said, "but are you sure you can handle it with Nancy and everything?"

"I doubt it, but that's not going to stop me," I said.

We got our food and didn't talk for a while. I could see her naked in the steam, and my mind wandered into the future. I imagined having an affair with Jennifer and trying to keep it a secret. This was a major rock in the stream, and it scared me.

"What about Rich?" I said.

"What about him?" she said.

"I thought you two were pretty serious," I said.

"I think I like you better," she said. "I'm not married. I'm a free woman."

"That's what I wanted to hear," I said.

"I want to have an affair with you, though, not just a one-night stand," she said.

"That's what I want, too," I said. "I think I'm in love with you."

"Take it easy, lover," she said. "Let's take this one step at a time."

"I'm sorry. I'm overwhelmed with emotion," I said.

"Be cool, brother. You have nothing to worry about," she said.

"I'm glad you're calm," I said, "but then you're not exactly cheating."

"I'm cheating, too," she said.

We finished our food, and I told her I would call her later. After I left the restaurant, I had a terrible feeling of dread. I thought about Nancy, and how I was doing something that I had never dreamed of doing. I was deeply infatuated with Jennifer though, and I knew I was going to go through with it. The feeling of dread passed quickly as I thought about fucking Jennifer. I went home and found that Nancy was out. I got on the exercise bicycle and rode for about twenty minutes. After I got all pumped up, I didn't know what to do with myself. I didn't want Nancy to come back, but I also wanted her to. I didn't realize what tricks my conscience would play on me by thinking about cheating. I changed my mind several times by the time Nancy arrived.

"Hi. Where have you been?" I said.

"I went to the store to buy some food. Do you want to help me with the bags?" she said.

"Sure," I said.

"How was your lunch with Greg?" she said.

"Fine," I said.

"What was he talking about?" she said.

"His kids mostly. They're still doing pretty well," I said.

"How's his wife?" she said.

"She's fine too," I said.

I didn't feel comfortable lying to her, and suddenly I had doubts about getting together with Jennifer. After putting away the groceries, I felt like getting away from Nancy.

"I'm going for a short walk," I said, bringing the phone with me.

I went outside and looked up at the sky. It was cloudy with gaps of blue. I wanted to call Jennifer but thought it was too soon. The conversation at lunch echoed in my mind. I couldn't believe how forward she had been, and how I had responded. I liked her assertiveness but felt she was in charge, which was new to me. Nancy and I were equals, and we didn't try to control each other. I decided to call Jennifer.

"Hey," she said, "I can't stop thinking about you."

"Same here," I said.

"When are we going to get together?" she said.

"Slow down a bit. This is more complicated than it looks," I said.

"I know. I'm sorry," she said.

"I actually thought I was going to have to talk you into it. I didn't know you were thinking the same thing I was," I said.

"I was flirting with you pretty heavily out in the woods," she said. "I'm surprised you didn't notice."

"I did notice, but I thought it was my imagination playing tricks on me," I said. "Listen. I'd better go back home. I'll call you tomorrow."

"Okay. Bye," she said.

It was starting to drizzle out, as was typical of Syracuse weather. I was hoping that Nancy wasn't getting suspicious. It was odd for me to go for a walk for the hell of it. When I got home, Nancy was reading in her favorite chair.

"Hi, sweetheart," she said. "It's starting to rain out, isn't it?"

"Yeah. I didn't get much exercise," I said.

"What do you want for dinner?" she said.

"Maybe we could order pizza," I said.

"That's fine with me," she said.

I felt so guilty. I felt uncomfortable being around her, so I went and sat in the den to read. I kept thinking about Jennifer and imagining making love to her. I could hardly think about having a baby with Nancy, but I was going to go through with that too.

"Let's make love before we order the pizza," she said.

"Can we do it afterwards?" I said.

"No. Come on," she said.

"All right," I said.

We went into the bedroom, and I imagined being with Jennifer. We made love, and I came inside her. That made her happy. When I thought about it, it didn't take very much to make her happy, but often I wasn't even able to do that. It still scared me to have a baby with her, especially since I was so infatuated with Jennifer. We ordered the pizza and sat in the living room listening to some jazz.

"I think I'm really pregnant," Nancy said.

"How do you know?"

"I was supposed to get my period yesterday, and I haven't gotten it yet. You know how regular I am."

"That's great," I said, without enthusiasm.

"You don't sound too excited," she said.

"It's a surprise. That's all. I didn't think it would happen this soon."

"Well, it's happening," she said.

"What do we have to do now?" I said.

"I'm going to the doctor's tomorrow," she responded. "Then we'll see what he says."

"Should I tell anyone?" I said.

"Not yet. You're happy, aren't you?"

"Yes. I'm happy," I said.

"Good, because I'm very content right now," she said.

The pizza came and we ate. I couldn't get Jennifer out of my mind. I didn't know what attracted her to me, but I decided to simply accept it. I knew I was in a lot of trouble. Now I wasn't looking forward to having a child and wished I hadn't made Nancy pregnant. I went to bed early, and Nancy stayed up to read. I dreamt about Jennifer, about making love in the woods. After we made love though, she chased me through the forest with a knife in her hands, right into the arms of Nancy. I woke up with a start and found Nancy sleeping next to me. I went out into the kitchen and made half a pot of coffee. I sat there thinking and stared at the refrigerator. I knew I couldn't go back to sleep, so I drank some coffee and thought about Jennifer and Nancy. I really didn't want to hurt Nancy. I had to keep my affair a secret. I projected into the future and imagined sleeping with Jennifer two or three times a week. Nancy apparently noticed that I wasn't in bed, and she came out into the kitchen.

"What's the matter?" she asked.

"I had a bad dream," I said.

"Are you all right now?"

"I'm fine. I can't sleep is all," I said.

"Are you worried about something?" she said.

"Like what?" I said.

"Like having a baby," she said.

"Not at all," I said.

"Well, there must be something wrong. You don't usually suffer from nightmares," she said.

"It's probably the pizza," I said.

"I'm going back to bed," she said.

"I'll join you in a while," I said.

I sat there feeling guilty but still thinking about Jennifer. I decided to call her in the middle of the night. I went down into the basement with my phone and dialed the number. She didn't answer the first time, so I called again.

"Hello?" she said sleepily.

"Hi, sweetheart," I said.

"What's wrong?" she said.

"I can't stop thinking about you," I said.

"Can't you wait to call me in the morning?" she said.

"Of course I can. I'm sorry," I said and hung up.

I felt like a fool and went back upstairs. I sat in the kitchen and drank some more coffee. I didn't want to go right to bed, so I stayed up and thought about what an ass I had made out of myself. My thoughts were fumbled, and I thought it probably wasn't a good idea to get together with Jennifer. Then I thought I couldn't resist her, and I hated being so confused. I gave up and went to bed. I tossed and turned for a while, waking Nancy up.

"Can't sleep?" she said.

"No. I'm going to go in the other room so I don't disturb you," I said.

I went into the guest room and lay down with my eyes wide open. Since I had drunk so much coffee, there was no way I was going to sleep. I hated being tired and not able to sleep. I had terrible thoughts and went into the bathroom to take a sleeping pill. Finally, I slept.

Chapter 4

I woke up late, still groggy from the sleeping pill. I heard Nancy in the kitchen, then remembered calling Jennifer in the middle of the night. I showered and shaved, then went into the kitchen.

"Did you get enough sleep?" Nancy said.

"I guess so," I said, "but I don't like the way those sleeping pills make me feel in the morning."

"I don't either," she said.

"I'm going to paint today. I'm determined," I said.

"Good, I'm going for my walk," she said.

After she left, I decided to call Jennifer and apologize for calling her so late at night.

"Hi," she said.

"Sorry about last night," I said.

"That's all right. I was kind of flattered that you're thinking about me so much," she said.

"I think about you constantly now," I said.

"Me too. I think about myself all the time." She laughed.

"When can we get together again?" I said.

"Anytime you want," she said.

"Maybe I can get away for an hour this evening," I said.

"Call me later and let me know," she said.

After I hung up, I had this sudden pang of guilt. Nancy came back from her walk, and I went right into the studio. I sat there in front of the blank canvas for half an hour. Finally, I came out.

"How's it going?" she asked.

"Not very well. I can't come up with an idea," I said.

"Have a cup of coffee and relax. Something will come to you," she said.

"Are you going to paint today, too?" I said.

"No. I'm going to write a poem," she said.

"That's unusual for you," I said.

"I thought I'd try it, expand my horizons," she said.

"I'm going to my mother's tonight for an hour," I said. "I haven't seen her for a long time."

"That's nice," she said.

I was glad I got away with that one, but I wondered how often I could make excuses to get away. I figured I would go over to my mother's for about fifteen minutes and then meet up with Jennifer.

"What are you going to write about?" I said.

"Disillusionment," she said.

"That's interesting," I said. "What kind?"

"About men and women in relationships," she said.

"Ours?" I said.

"Yes."

"Are you disillusioned?" I said.

"Isn't everybody?" she said.

"I thought you were excited about having the baby?"

"I am," she said, "but you're not."

"I am, but maybe not as much as you," I said.

"Then why don't you talk about it?" she said.

"What am I supposed to say? We're having a kid."

"That's exactly what I mean," she said.

56

"Don't take that the wrong way," I said. "I love our little baby."

"You don't have to fake it for me," she said.

"I'm not arguing anymore," I said and left the room.

I went into the studio and sat on my chair, angry at her and myself. I was uncomfortable and didn't know what to do. I decided to paint, and I used fierce red and black colors. The painting didn't turn out well, and I threw it out. I was used to painting with deep blues and greens, highlighted by bright yellows and reds. I decided to call Jennifer and make an appointment.

"Hi. What's up?" she said.

"I can come over later, but only for an hour," I said.

"That's fine. It'll be quality time." She laughed. "What time?"

"About seven," I said.

"Okay. Bye."

I had the sudden feeling of elation, and my anger quickly disappeared. I sat down to do another small painting and simply did a sunset over a calm ocean. It turned out well, and I showed it to Nancy, who was still working on the poem.

"Oh, it's great!" she said.

"I like it too," I said. "How's your poem going?"

"It's churning like a resentment, but I'm glad I'm putting it on paper. That way it doesn't stay in my head."

"You can talk to me about it," I said.

"Maybe later."

"I don't want you to have a resentment against me," I said.

"I don't as of yet."

"Well, don't get one," I said.

"We need to do something to spice up our marriage," she said.

"Like what?"

"Like a trip to Italy," she said. "It's been a long time since we've been there."

"Before you deliver the baby?" I said.

"Of course not. Afterwards."

"It's all right with me. When exactly do you want to go?"

"I thought next month," she said.

"Okay. I'll make the arrangements. We should go to Rome to see Allesandre," I said.

I thought immediately that this trip would interfere with my affair with Jennifer. I couldn't wait until that evening. Nancy went to her doctor's appointment, and I sat down to do some writing. I couldn't concentrate, naturally, and gave up after a while. I ate something and had a cup of coffee. I called my mother and told her I would be over at about six-thirty. Nancy came back an hour later and said she was fine.

"What do we have to do?" I said.

"I have to take care of myself is all," she said, "and you have to take care of me, too."

"I will," I said. "I'm going to take a nap now."

"Okay," she said. "What do you want for dinner?"

"Pork chops," I said.

I went into our bedroom and lay down. I couldn't sleep though, because I was too excited about that evening. I stayed there for a long time, with my eyes wide open, fantasizing. I got up when Nancy called me for dinner.

"Smells good," I said. "What are we having with them?"

"Broccoli and baked potato," she said.

We ate, and I was unusually silent, which I was sure Nancy noticed. I was thinking terrible thoughts, and finally one came out.

"I'm not sure we should have this baby," I said.

"What!" she screamed.

"I don't think it's the right time," I said.

"I can't believe this," she said. "When do you think the right time is going to be? I'm keeping this baby. You can go to hell!"

She stormed out of the room and left me feeling like an ass. I sat there, without moving, thinking of what to do next. I decided to get in my car and go for a long drive. I drove and drove out into the countryside and thought about what had just happened. I had finally spoken the truth and was willing to pay the consequences. I felt like I was going over a waterfall. I wanted to be with Jennifer, so I called her.

"Hey, what's up?" she said.

"Can I meet you now?" I said.

"Sure. Come on over. I just got home," she said.

I had a mixture of feelings. I felt guilty and angry, confused and excited, all at the same time. I was mostly excited though, and all I could think about was fucking Jennifer. It took me about twenty minutes to make it to her place, and she welcomed me at the door in a negligee.

"Hi," she said.

"Don't you look hot," I said.

"It's some old thing I threw on," she said laughing. "Come on in."

I walked into a beautiful apartment. It was small but cozy.

"I know you don't drink, so I made you some coffee," she

said. "I thought you were coming over later."

"I had a fight with Nancy," I said. "I told her I didn't want a child yet. She's pregnant."

"That couldn't have gone over too well," she said.

"It didn't, but I finally said what I really feel."

"What is she going to do?"

"I have no idea. Probably leave me and keep the child," I said.

"But you love her, don't you?"

"Yes," I said, "but I love you too."

"You don't know if you love me yet," she said.

"I have strong feelings for you, as strong as those for Nancy," I said.

That made me feel better. For a second, I didn't know how she felt. I knew she wanted to have sex with me, but I wanted her to feel something too. I smiled and put my head down. This was the perfect opening for a sexual advance, and I was going to take it.

"Do you want to show me your bedroom?" I said.

"Sure. Come on," she said.

We walked into this small room with a huge, king-sized bed in it. I laughed at the proportions.

"Everyone has to have their priorities," she said with a laugh.

"Lie down," I said. "I'll give you a backrub."

"Okay."

She took her shirt off and stretched out on the bed. I rubbed her back gently, and then increased the pressure. She moaned with pleasure, and I started rubbing her ass. She rolled over and I began massaging her breasts. The next thing you know, we were naked and writhing around. She put her mouth on my cock and went up and down slowly. She was a master at giving head, but I couldn't keep it up.

"You have too much on your mind," she said.

"I'm sorry, honey. Let me lick you," I said.

I licked her pussy and made her come. That made her feel better. I was disappointed that I couldn't fuck her, but I was glad I had broken the ice. Suddenly, I realized I had to go back to Nancy and felt guilty as hell. I was very uncomfortable being in Jennifer's apartment and excused myself to leave. I left hastily, but Jennifer seemed to understand. When I got home, Nancy was out. I sat down at the kitchen table and tried to relax. My body was swirling with various emotions, none of them good. I thought I would never cheat on Nancy again. A while later, Nancy came home.

"Where have you been," I said.

"I went over to my mother's," she said.

"She must hate me too now," I said.

"We don't hate you," she said, "but pretty close."

"I'm sorry, honey. I didn't mean what I said. I want to have the baby.

"How can you change your mind so suddenly?" she said.

"This is difficult for me," I simply said.

"I don't understand how every other man in this world can have children without any problem, but not you," she said.

"That's not true," I said. "Lots of men have problems like that."

"I'm going to bed. I'm not going to fight anymore tonight," she said. "We'll see how tomorrow goes."

"Fine. I'll sleep on the couch," I said.

"Good idea," she said.

She went to bed, and I got the couch ready for the night. I was miserable. I felt guilty, but suddenly remembered licking Jennifer and thought how nice it had been. The couch was uncomfortable, and I tossed and turned for two hours. I got some sleep but woke up at five, as miserable as before. Nancy hadn't slept at all either. The echo from the day before was very painful. I was confused and didn't know how to handle it. I made some coffee and sat, slumped over, at the kitchen table. Nancy came out a while later and sat next to me.

"You don't look too well," she said.

"I feel awful," I said.

"Maybe you need to see a therapist," she said.

"I think that's a good idea," I said. "I'm very confused."

I felt like confessing about Jennifer but wisely decided against it. There was no reason to hurt her more. I had already done enough damage.

"I'm going to call Greg and see if he knows someone I can see," I said.

I called Greg, and he referred me to a psychologist nearby. I called the office and made an appointment for the following week.

"Is it a man or a woman?" Nancy asked.

"It's a man," I said.

"Well, I hope he can give you some insights into your problems," she said.

"I hope so too."

"Why don't you go back to bed," she said.

"Okay."

I went back to bed and fell right to sleep. I woke up three

hours later and felt better. I was still feeling guilty and angry at myself. I went out into the kitchen and poured myself a cup of cold coffee. I put some ice cubes into it and drank it cold. Nancy was in the studio.

"What are you working on?" I said.

"My poem," she said. "It's turning out better than I thought."

"I'm glad. I hope I'm not in it though," I said.

"You are, sort of," she said.

"Are you making me into a villain?" I said.

"You made yourself into one," she said, "but I took it easy on you. I made you human."

I made myself a sandwich and left Nancy alone. I wanted to call Jennifer. She made me feel love, and I was having strong feelings for her, even though I felt guilty. I went for a walk and called Jennifer.

"How are you?" she said.

"Not good," I said.

"You didn't tell her, did you?" she said.

"No," I said.

"Good," she said.

"I want to see you," I said.

"I can't get away until later. Can you come over about eight?" she said.

"I'll try. I'll call you later," I said.

That made me feel better. At least Jennifer wanted to be with me. I walked for a while. I could smell the coming of winter. It was a cold day out. I had all kinds of negative thoughts running through my mind. I wondered what this therapist could possibly say to me that would change my thoughts or behavior. I went home and sat in front of the TV, not paying any attention. Nancy sat next to me and gave me a kiss on the cheek.

"I still love you," she said.

"That's good, because I was starting to wonder," I said.

"I wonder if you love me," she said.

"Of course I do. I've simply been thrown off by this child. That's all," I said.

"We can work through that," she said.

"I think so too," I said.

"Why don't we take a nice hot bath together, like we used to," she said.

"Okay."

We took a bath together and touched each other lovingly, without making love. It was great, but I couldn't stop thinking about Jennifer. I wanted to have sex with Jennifer and stay married to Nancy, the thought of which was driving me crazy.

"I want this baby," I said.

"You'll change your mind again," she said.

"I don't think so," I said.

We got out of the tub and dried off. I wanted to reassure her that I still loved her but knew my words didn't mean anything. I was sleepy so I lay down in the bed and closed my eyes. Instantly, the vision of Jennifer naked came into my mind. I had to make an excuse to get out of the house later, so I started thinking. I figured I would tell Nancy that I needed to go for a drive to clear my head. I knew it was a lame excuse, but I couldn't think of anything else. After a while, I fell asleep. I dreamt about Jennifer. We were out in the woods and stumbled upon a small pond. She wanted to go swimming, but I didn't want to go. She took her clothes off and jumped in. She couldn't swim, so I jumped in after her and pulled her ashore, giving her mouth-to-mouth resuscitation. She came back to life and simply walked away into the darkness. I woke up and tried to understand the significance of the dream but couldn't. I walked out to the kitchen, where Nancy was having a cup of coffee and looking through a magazine.

"I love you," I said. "I know we're going through a tough time right now, but I think our love is strong enough to endure."

"I know you love me. You're having doubts. That's all. It's normal," she said.

"Thanks for being so understanding," I said.

"I'm not that thrilled with you right now," she said, "but I'm trying to put things in perspective," she said.

"I've never been good at making decisions or taking responsibility," I said, "but I'm going to try harder!"

"That's all I can ask," she said.

"I'm going for a drive to clear my head," I said.

"Okay," she said.

I got into the car and immediately began to fantasize about Jennifer. After a few minutes of driving, I called her.

"Hey," she said.

"Hey yourself," I said. "I'm fine now, if you want to get together."

"Meet me at my place in twenty minutes," she said.

I drove over to her apartment and parked down the street a ways. I waited until I saw her pull up her driveway. I walked down the street and looked around as I went up to her door.

"Come on in," she said.

I felt like a criminal. I walked in and she gave me a big kiss on the lips.

"I think I just want to talk," I said.

"What's the matter?" she said.

"Nothing. I mean I feel guilty, and I'm not sure how to handle it," I said.

"I understand, but what we have is real. It's not only sex," she said.

"I know. I really do love you, but I also love Nancy, and we're about to have a child. I don't know what to do."

"Why don't we slow it down and spend some time together, and then see how we feel?" she said.

" Good idea," I said.

"Well, what should we talk about?" she said.

"I don't know. Everything, I guess," I said.

"Let's talk about our possible future," she said.

"I love you, but I don't know if I want to divorce Nancy to be with you. That's the truth."

"Hold on. Nobody's talking about divorce. I simply want to be with you. I don't need a piece of paper to prove that you love me," she said.

"I'm glad you said that, because I want to be with you, too. I simply don't know how this is going to work out," I said.

"I'm willing to share you," she said.

"What about Richard?" I said.

"I'm going to break up with him," she said.

"That's good," I said.

I wanted to touch her skin and slowly take her clothes off. She had such cute expressions, and her pouty lips were driving me wild.

"I want to fuck you," I finally said.

"I want to fuck you, too," she said.

We went into the bedroom and jumped on the bed. We kissed for a long time. Her lips were so soft. I immediately got hard. I took her shirt off and then her bra. I massaged her breasts while kissing her very tenderly. I felt like I was in love. She took my pants off and began sucking my cock. I watched her lips go up and down on me and was hard as a rock. I thought about Nancy, but I quickly put her out of my mind. I fucked Jennifer ever so hard and came inside her, which I didn't mean to do.

"It's all right. I'm not at the peak of my cycle," she said.

"Still, I shouldn't have done it," I said.

"Don't worry about it. I'll take a pill," she said. "Do you feel guilty now?"

"Yes. A little. But I wanted to do it," I said.

"I guess you'll have to live with the guilt," she said.

"Do you feel guilty?" I said.

"Not at all," she said. "Why should I?"

"Because you're hurting Nancy, too," I said.

"I'm not into guilt trips," she said.

"You're lucky, or cruel," I said.

"I'm not cruel," she said. "It's a competitive world, and I'm doing my best to compete. Besides, you got hard this time. You can't be feeling too guilty."

"I feel guilty enough," I said.

I wanted to leave. The more I talked about it, the worse I felt. I told Jennifer I would call her the next day, and I walked out. I felt like I was caught in a circling pool of water. I reflected on what I had just done and felt nauseous. I got in the car and drove straight home.

"That was a long drive," Nancy said.

"Yeah. I went out to route twenty, drove through Cazenovia, and all the way out to the lake," I said.

"Do you feel better?" she said.

"A bit, I guess," I said.

"Are you hungry?" she said.

"Not really. I'll eat later," I said.

I went right to the bedroom and lay down. I thought about making love to Jennifer and felt even more guilty. I wanted to sleep but couldn't. I knew that Nancy would want to have sex that night, and I had to come up with some excuse not to. It was getting more complicated all the time, and I felt like I had to make a decision. I either had to stay with Nancy or make a commitment to Jennifer. Nancy came into the bedroom to see how I was doing.

"How do you feel, sweetheart?" she said.

"Not very well," I said.

"Maybe we should go to therapy together," she said.

"Whatever you want," I said.

"I think it would be better for our communication to see someone together," she said. "There are a lot of things I want to say but can't say."

"That's fine. We'll go together," I said, thinking that I wouldn't be able to divulge anything I really wanted to.

Apparently, she knew better than to ask me for sex. I closed my eyes and tried to sleep again. I went into a half sleep that felt like I was living in a dream. I dreamt that I was walking through the woods naked with Jennifer. Nancy came upon us and began fighting with Jennifer. I tried to break it up but got tangled in the fight, which turned into a sexual threesome. I woke up and was distraught. I knew what the dream meant. It was an internal struggle for me between the two women. I got up and went out into the kitchen where Nancy was sitting.

"I had a bad dream," I said.

"What about?" she said.

"We were fighting," I said, "physically."

"Don't worry about it," she said.

"I hate fighting, or even dreaming about it," I said.

"It's only a dream," she said.

"But dreams mean something," I said.

"They're like fiction, open to interpretation," she said.

"I know, but this one's fairly obvious," I said.

"I guess you're right. You have some inner turmoil that only you can resolve, maybe with outside help," she said.

"I've never felt this way before. It's foreign territory," I said.

"I haven't felt this way before either," she said.

"I'm going to sleep," I said.

"I'll leave you alone," she said.

Chapter 5

I took a pill, and twenty minutes later, I fell asleep. I was so exhausted from my adventures that I slept all the way through the night, but with some terrible dreams. I woke up feeling groggy from the pill, so I went into the kitchen and made some coffee. Nancy was still sleeping, and I didn't wake her. After the first cup of coffee, I felt better, but the bad dreams echoed in my memory. I thought for a minute that I should end my relationship with Jennifer. Then I thought I couldn't give her up. I went in the basement and called Jennifer.

"Hey," she said, "how are you feeling?"

"Not that great, but I have to see you," I said.

"When?" she said.

As soon as possible," I said.

"I can get away in an hour," she said. "I'll meet you then."

I got in the car and took off before Nancy woke up. I would figure out an excuse later. I drove out into the country. I would have to kill some time before I went over to Jennifer's. I didn't know what to say to her. I thought I should break it off with her, but I wanted to fuck her in the worst way. I drove quickly and went past the speed limit. I had the music blaring, and I couldn't think. I slowed down after a while and made my way to Jennifer's place. She was waiting for me.

"Hi," she said. "You sounded pretty upset."

"Yeah, this affair is driving me crazy," I said.

"I can't help it," she said. "It's what we both want."

"I know it. I'm not ready to give you up," I said.

I walked into the kitchen with her, and she gave me a cup of coffee.

"I can't stay long," I said.

"I know. I have to go back to work, too," she said. "Do you want to talk or make love?"

"I want to make love," I said.

"Me too," she said.

We got on the bed with all our clothes on and simply kissed for a long time. We undressed each other slowly and made love tenderly. I finally felt relaxed, as I put all thoughts of Nancy out of my mind. Afterwards, we took a shower together, and thoughts of Nancy rushed back into my mind.

"I have to go," I said, after dressing.

"I'll talk to you later," she said.

I drove to the store and bought a few things, so that I would have an excuse to tell Nancy. When I got home, she was in the studio, painting.

"Hi," I said.

"Where have you been?" she said.

"I went to my mother's for a minute. Then I went to the store," I said.

"How's your mom?" she said.

"Fine," I said. "Oh, that looks nice so far."

"Yeah, I like it too," she said. "How do you feel today?"

"Not so great," I said. "I had some bad dreams last night. They scared me."

"Do you need to rest some more?" she asked.

"Not yet, I don't think, but I need to relax," I said.

I went into the living room and put on some music. I loved to listen to Miles Davis when I was stressed out, and this was one of those times. I went back and forth from thinking about Nancy, and then Jennifer. I knew I couldn't keep this up, but I didn't know what to do. My rational side thought I should drop Jennifer, but my passionate side thought I should give up Nancy. I couldn't relax. The music flowed over me as I stretched out on the couch and closed my eyes. In my imagination, I made love to Jennifer, kissing her soft skin and her tender lips. I was in love with her. I imagined fishing in the stream with Jennifer naked next to me. I wanted to escape. Nancy came into the living room after a while, taking a break from her painting.

"Do you feel more relaxed now?" she said.

"A little bit," I said. "There's something I have to tell you."

"Oh no, here we go," she said.

"I think I should see a therapist by myself," I said.

"Is that all? That's fine," she said.

"Because I want to tell him my deepest thoughts," I said.

"I understand," she said. "I'm going back to paint."

I wanted to call Jennifer, so I went out for a walk and called her two blocks from our house.

"I bet you're feeling good," Jennifer said.

"Not really. I miss you," I said.

"Can you get away this evening?" she asked.

"I don't think so, but I'll try," I said. "I only called to say hi. I'll call you later."

"Okay, bye," she said.

It was a cool day again, and I had gone out without a jacket. I went right back home, hoping not to see Nancy right away. I had gotten a chill by the time I walked in the door, but I was glad Nancy was still in the studio. I sat down in the kitchen for a minute, then decided to make a pot of coffee. The hot coffee tasted good, but I still wasn't able to relax. Nancy came out and poured herself a cup.

"I finished. Do you want to see it?" she asked.

"Sure," I said.

"We walked into the studio, and I saw the darkest painting I had ever seen her do. It was a painting of a shipwreck at night.

"What do you think?" she said.

"I like it," I said. "The darkness is intense."

"Yeah, I like it too," she said. "I think it's one of my better ones."

"You should be able to sell that for a thousand dollars," I said.

"I hope so," she said.

I didn't have to think too long about where she had gotten the idea for the painting, but I wasn't going to discuss it with her. She obviously thought our relationship was falling apart, and I knew it, too.

"I'm going shopping for groceries," she said, as she pulled the refrigerator open.

After she left, I called Jennifer again.

"I want to see you later," I said.

"Meet me at five," she said.

I was horny as hell after hearing Jennifer's voice. I wondered how long I would lust after her before becoming used to the sex and losing the passion. I had lost most of my urge for sex with Nancy, but I loved her, too. I left the house and went over to Greg's house to kill some time. My imagination was going wild. I had Jennifer in all kinds of positions. Greg was home alone. He was waiting for his wife and kids to return.

"What's going on, playboy?" he said.

"Don't say that," I said.

"Relax. I'm only kidding. I guess I hit a sore spot," he said.

"My life is a mess," I said, "and I don't know how to straighten it out."

"Talk to me," he said.

"I'm getting involved with Jennifer, and now I think I'm in love with her," I said.

"You haven't really given it enough time," he said.

"I know, but I like everything about her, and the sex is intense," I said.

"You know the sex is going to wear off, and you still love Nancy. Don't you?" he said.

"Yes, I still love Nancy. That's why I don't know what to do," I said.

"I don't know what to tell you. I think you should stick to Nancy now that she's pregnant and everything," he said.

"That's what kills me. It was such bad timing," I said.

"Is there any good timing when it comes to these things?" he said.

"I guess not," I said. I'm supposed to meet up with Jennifer in a little while. I don't know what to say to her."

"I already told you what I think," he said.

"Thanks. I appreciate it," I said. "I'll talk to you later."

I left Greg's house and drove over to Jennifer's. I was trying to think of an excuse to tell Nancy. I figured I'd tell her I was at Greg's. When I got to Jennifer's house, I noticed her car wasn't there, so I parked down the street and waited. Half an hour later, she showed up. I was excited but nervous at the same time. I followed her up to the door and she simply walked in, holding the door for me.

"I'm having somewhat of a difficult day at work today," she said. "One of my deals fell through."

"I'm sorry to hear that," I said. "I'm having a tough day, too."

"Maybe we can make each other feel better," she said.

"I want to talk," I said.

"Okay," she said.

"We have to slow this thing down. I don't want to end it, but it's too chaotic," I said.

"That's fine," she said.

"I want to be with you all the time, but it's not possible now," I said.

"I understand," she said. "It's a bit much for me, too."

I kissed her on the lips and felt like making love to her, but I resisted.

"I love you," I said.

"I love you too," she said.

"I have to go," I said. "I'll call you tomorrow."

"Bye, sweetheart," she said.

I drove home, wishing that I had fucked Jennifer, but I knew I had been better off not doing it. Nancy was waiting for me, and I told her I had been at Greg's house. She didn't question me, but I knew I had to visit Jenifer less often, so that Nancy wouldn't get suspicious.

"How do you feel?" Nancy said. "Did you have a nice talk with Greg?"

"Yeah, he's great," I said.

"What did you talk about?" she said.

"Mostly about his kids," I said.

"How are they?" she said.

"Oh, they're fine," I said.

I wanted to get right out of this conversation, so I told her I was tired and needed to lie down.

"I'll make us some pasta," she said.

"That's fine," I said.

I went into the bedroom and lay on the bed. All I could think about was being with Jennifer. I was uncomfortable no matter what I did, and I knew that I couldn't see Jennifer for a while. I fell asleep after a while and dreamt of being with Jennifer. It was a bad dream though, and I woke up with a start. I didn't realize I had been asleep for such a long time, and I wondered why Nancy hadn't awakened me. I could smell the pasta sauce cooking and went out to the kitchen.

"How did you sleep?" Nancy said.

"I had a bad dream again," I said.

"Your conscience must not be too clear," she said.

"What do you mean?" I said.

"You must be feeling guilty about something, having all these bad dreams," she said.

"I don't feel guilty about anything. That's not the only reason one has bad dreams," I said.

"What was this one about?" she said.

"I can't remember now," I said.

"Pleading the fifth?" she said.

She made the spaghetti, and we ate in silence. The guilt was eating me alive. The food tasted great. Nancy made a good sauce, but I couldn't help feeling that she suspected something.

Why would she bring up the subject of guilt over a bad dream? After we ate, I did the dishes, and she rubbed my shoulders. I hadn't made love to her in a long time, and I felt guilty about that, too. Now it was uncomfortable to talk. I had to do something, but I didn't know what.

"You haven't done any work in a few days," she said. "What's the matter?"

"I don't know. I don't feel inspired," I said.

"You told me once that art work had nothing to do with inspiration, that it was merely hard work," she said.

"Well, I haven't felt like working," I said.

"I understand that, but I think something is bothering you besides this child," she said.

"Like what?" I said.

"I don't know. That's what I'm asking," she said.

"Nothing else is bothering me," I said.

"Then I take it you don't want to have this baby," she said.

"I'm undecided," I said.

"Well, you'd better make up your mind," she said. "I'm having the baby no matter what!"

"I'm going for a drive," I said, thinking that I might call Jennifer.

I left the house feeling like shit. I got in the car and tore out of the driveway. I was tired, and it was getting late, but I still wanted to talk to Jennifer. I called her.

"Hey," she said.

"Hey yourself," I said. "I had an argument with Nancy."

"I'd like to say I'm sorry, but I don't feel that way," she said.

"Can I see you?" I said.

"Not tonight. Tomorrow," she said. "I'm going to bed early."

Okay. I'll call you tomorrow," I said.

I drove around for a while, not wanting to go home. Finally, I pulled up into the driveway. All the lights in the house were off. The door was unlocked, and I noticed a blanket and pillow on the couch. I didn't want to sleep with Nancy anyway, so I lay down on the couch and went to sleep. I didn't fall asleep right away. I tossed and turned for about an hour. I had a nightmare about Nancy stabbing me in the back while I was sleeping, and I woke up in the middle of the night. I dragged my ass out to the kitchen and had a cup of tea. Nancy heard me and came out to see me.

"Are you all right?" she said.

"Not really. I had another nightmare," I said.

"I'm glad you're getting some professional help. Maybe you should go on some medication," she said.

"I don't know what they could put me on, maybe an anti-depressant," I said. "I'm going to try to go back to sleep."

"You can sleep in the bed with me," she said.

We went back to bed, and lying next to Nancy felt better. I fell right to sleep. I slept till nine-thirty, which was late for me, and Nancy was already up in the kitchen. I poured myself a cup of coffee and gave Nancy a kiss on the cheek. Her hair was pulled back in a pony tail. She hadn't showered yet.

"I think I might get a job," Nancy said.

"Really? What brought that on?" I said.

"I don't know. I only paint for two hours or so a day. I need to keep myself busier," she said.

"What kind of job?" I said.

"I was thinking of working in an art gallery," she said.

"That might be nice," I said. "I have a connection. Maybe I can get you in."

"That's what I was hoping," she said.

"I'll call my friend Josh today," I said.

Josh was a local art dealer who had been my friend since we were kids.

"Now I'm getting excited," she said.

"I hope it works out," I said, thinking that Nancy's job would give me an opportunity to spend more time with Jennifer.

"I also need to take my mind off of you," she said.

"I understand," I said. "I'm going for a walk."

I put on some clothes and went outside, bringing my phone with me. I called Jennifer, who was already at work.

"Hi," she said.

"How did you sleep last night?" I said.

"Fine. Why?" she said.

"I've been having nightmares," I said.

"That's terrible. Is there anything I can do to help?" she said.

"Keep loving me," I said.

"You can count on that," she said. "Do you want to get together today?"

"Yeah. Let me call you when I can get free," I said.

I walked back home and decided I would write a bit of poetry. Nancy was busy painting, and I sat behind her at our desk. I thought I would write about the woods and the beautiful pond set in the hills. I felt like I was being pushed against a rock in the middle of a stream, but I tried to keep my composure and write a peaceful poem. I wrote about canoeing on the lake with a woman and tipping the canoe by accident. We both got wet, and she got angry. The poem didn't turn out as peaceful as I had hoped.

"How's the painting going?" I said.

"Pretty well," she said. "This one's a lot brighter."

"You must be in a better mood," I said.

"I guess so," she said.

"My writing is horrible today," I said.

"I'm not surprised, the way you've been sleeping," she said.

"I can usually block out everything and write whatever I want, but not today," I said.

"Don't worry about it," she said. I'll be done in another hour or so."

"Okay, I'm going to make myself something to eat," I said.

"There's some time," she said.

I went into the kitchen and tried to relax. I couldn't stop thinking about Jennifer and Nancy with the baby. I was usually good about making decisions, but now I was caught in a serious dilemma. I made myself a sandwich and ate very slowly. I hadn't made love to Nancy in a while, and I knew it was bothering her. Now that I was fucking Jennifer, I had no desire to make love to Nancy. I told Nancy that I was going over to my mother's house, and that I wouldn't be back for a few hours. I thought this would give me enough time to get together with Jennifer. I got in the car and drove over to my mother's, calling Jennifer on the way.

"Hey," she said.

"Are you working?" I said.

"Yes, but I can get away in an hour," she said.

80

"I'll meet you then," I said.

I drove on and went to my mother's. I usually talked to her about what was going on with me, but I couldn't this day. We sat for an hour and chit-chatted, but there was nothing of substance. Afterwards, I went over to Jennifer's and waited for her to pull up in her driveway. She showed up about ten minutes later.

"Come on in," she said.

"I don't have much time," I said.

"I'm sorry about those nightmares," she said.

"I feel so guilty, but I can't stop myself," I said.

"There's nothing I can say that won't make you feel guilty, but I want you to be with me," she said.

"I want to be with you too, but I can't let go of Nancy," I said.

"Our sex is better, isn't it?" she said.

"Yes, yes it is," I said, "but the love is the same."

"Well, you'll get to love me more as time goes on," she said. "Now let's make love."

She took off her clothes as she walked into the bedroom, and I followed her. I let her take my clothes off, and we made love for an hour. I was so excited I came twice. We lay there afterwards, exhausted, and talked intimately.

"I want you to marry me," she said.

"I can't do anything now," I said.

"Can't you get a divorce?" she said.

"Not yet," I said. "The baby's coming, and I don't know what I want to do."

"I'll give you as much time as you need," she said.

"Thanks," I said.

"But I'm not going to wait forever," she said.

"I don't expect you to," I said.

"I love you, but I know how these things go. I'm not going to let you string me along forever," she said.

"I'm going to make a decision, one way or the other," I said.

"As long as we keep making love like this, I know what decision you'll make," she said.

"I appreciate your waiting for me," I said. "I have to go now."

I dressed and kissed her goodbye. I drove back to my house, and Nancy was home cooking soup.

"How's your mom?" she said.

"She's fine. Her bridge game is better than ever," I said.

"I need to talk to you," she said.

"What's up?" I said.

"If you want to split up, I'll understand, but I need to know," she said.

"I don't want to split up," I said. "I'm going through a difficult time is all."

"I'm thinking maybe I should be on my own," she said.

"And take care of the baby by yourself?" I said.

"If I have to," she said. "I can't be with someone who can't commit to me."

"Let's not make any rash decisions," I said. "Give me a chance to get used to the idea."

"I'll give you some time, but I'm not going to wait forever," she said.

"Let's talk about this another time," I said.

"That's all I wanted to say," she said.

I went into the bedroom and stretched out on the bed. I closed my eyes, and instantly the image of making love to Jennifer came into my mind. I imagined being married to her, and the passion we could generate. Then I thought about after the passion faded, and how it would become routine like it was with Nancy. I decided to call Greg and bounce a few things off of him. I closed the bedroom door and called him.

"Hey, bro," he said.

"How are you?" I said.

"I'm probably calmer than you," he said.

"You're right about that," I said.

"What's up?" he said.

"I'm in a terrible dilemma," I said.

"I know you are," he said.

"I've got to make a decision soon. Both women are putting pressure on me," I said.

"Does Nancy know about Jennifer yet?" he said.

"No," I said.

"Well, don't tell her," he said.

"I'm not going to," I said, "but I can't keep going on the way I'm going."

"I already told you, break it off with Jennifer," he said.

"I can't," I said.

"I gave you my advice. There's no more I can tell you," he said.

"Thanks. I'll talk to you later," I said.

After I hung up, I lay back down on the bed, and Jennifer's naked body came back into my imagination. I couldn't control it. I felt like I was being pushed downstream with no way to get to the shore.

Chapter 6

I was afraid to face Nancy again, but I went into the kitchen anyway. She was reading a book, and the soup smelled good. I made a pot of coffee and sat next to her.

"How do you feel?" she said.

"Not great," I said.

"You've completely lost your sense of humor," she said.

"I know, and it's killing me," I said.

"It hurts me, too," she said. "We used to have so much fun."

"We will again, after I get better," I said.

"But what's it going to take for you to get better?" she said.

"Time," I said.

"I don't see that," she said.

We ate some soup with bread and were silent for a while. It was an uncomfortable silence, and Nancy had a disgruntled look on her face. I wanted to tell her about Jennifer, if only to relieve the guilt, but held back. I thought that if Nancy knew I was having an affair, the relationship would be over.

"I'm going to my mother's tonight," Nancy said.

"Why?" I said.

"Because she's more enjoyable than you," she said.

"Fine," I said.

She got her things together and left. I quickly thought that I might see Jennifer again. I called her.

"Hey, what's up? I didn't expect to hear from you tonight?" she said.

Nancy went to her mother's. She's not too happy with me," I said.

"Do you want to get together again?" she said.

"I do, but I have to warn you, I'm not in a good mood," I said.

"I'll put you I a good mood," she said.

"Okay. I'll be over in a little while," I said.

I drove over to Jennifer's apartment and kept thinking about different things that I would say to her. I heard Greg's voice in my mind, telling me to break it off with her. I wanted a resolution to the problem, but I was caught in the middle. When I got to the front door, she opened it, wearing nothing but panties. She was so hot.

"Get dressed," I said.

"You really are in a bad mood," she said.

"I only want to talk," I said.

She got dressed, while I waited in the kitchen, and then she made us some tea.

"You seem so troubled," she said.

"I am. I'm destroying my marriage, and I don't know what I have with you yet, so I'm at a loss," I said.

"You have everything with me. I asked you to marry me," she said.

"I know, but we haven't known each other long enough," I said.

"You said you loved me," she said.

I sipped my tea and simply shook my head. I didn't know what to say to her, or how to clear my confusion. I wanted to be with one of them, but was in love with both.

"I need to take a break," I said, "so I can think things over."

"Okay. That's fine. Can we talk on the phone?" she said.

"Sure," I said.

"Don't leave just yet. Let's make love first," she said.

"I can't," I said, putting on my jacket.

I left in a hurry, before I got more tempted, and drove right home. I was very surprised to see Nancy's car in the driveway. I thought of an excuse quickly and walked in the door.

"Where did you go?" she said.

"Over to Gregory's," I said.

"I called Greg. He didn't know where you were," she said calmly.

I didn't know what to say. I panicked.

"I went over to Jennifer's house. Nothing is going on. I needed a sentimental ear is all," I said.

"Jennifer!!? From the camping trip? You're having an affair!" she screamed.

"No, I'm not. I'm only talking to her as a friend," I said.

"Sure, I believe that!" she said. "You have to move out. I'm not going to take this."

"All right. I'll stay at my mother's," I said.

I left the house and called my mother on the way. I felt like I was drowning in the stream. I was afraid. I don't even remember driving over to my mother's. She welcomed me with open arms. I could do no wrong in her eyes, though she didn't know what was going on.

"What were you fighting about?" my mother said.

"About the baby. I'm not sure I want to have it," I said.

"Oh, that's too bad. I thought you had your heart set on it," she said.

"I'm scared about it. I don't know if I can take care of it properly. It's coming at a bad time. Nancy and I aren't doing very well," I said.

"I thought you and Nancy were all right," she said.

"We've been having problems recently," I said.

I didn't want to talk about it anymore. I certainly wasn't going to tell my mother that I was having an affair.

"I'm going to bed," I said.

"Goodnight, sweetheart," she said.

I hadn't slept at my mother's in a long time, but surprisingly, I slept very well. I didn't have any nightmares, and I woke up pretty refreshed. As soon as I woke though, bad feelings rushed in on me. I had terrible feelings of guilt toward Nancy. I thought I would have to rent an apartment, and that didn't suit me. My mother was already up when I went into the kitchen, and I poured myself a fresh cup of coffee.

"How did you sleep, honey?" she said.

"Pretty well, actually, but I don't feel so good now," I said.

"I don't want to interfere, but if you want to talk, I'll listen," she said.

"I don't want to talk about anything," I said.

"Have it your way, but keeping it bottled up won't help," she said.

"I'm having an affair," I said.

"An affair?" she said.

"Yes," I said.

"Oh, Paul, how could you?" she said.

"I didn't exactly plan it," I said.

"I thought you loved Nancy," she said.

"I do. That's why I feel so guilty," I said.

"Well, you'd better cut it out, or you'll be out on your ear," she said.

"Mom, you don't understand. I'm in love with both of them," I said.

"You can't have both," she said.

"I know," I said. "That's enough."

"You do what you want, but I don't support you on this. I'm on Nancy's side," she said.

"Okay. Okay," I said.

I decided to call Nancy to see what was going on. I was afraid to call her, but I thought I had better do it.

"Hi," she said. "I'm really upset. I can't talk to you now."

"All right," I said, and hung up.

I felt terrible, and I wanted to call Jennifer to get some love. I couldn't call in front of my mother, so I excused myself and went for a walk.

"Hi," she said. "Are you feeling better?"

"Not really, but I feel better talking to you," I said.

"What's going on?" she said.

"I told Nancy I was over at your house," I said. "It didn't go well."

"I'm glad you told her," Jennifer said.

"I think I'm going to have to find an apartment," I said.

"You can stay with me," she said.

"I don't think that's a good idea," I said.

"Why? It would be a lot cheaper, and we could be together," she said.

"I can't," I said.

"Suit yourself," she said, "but I'm not giving up on you."

"I'll talk to you later," I said.

I walked back to my mother's. It was pretty chilly out. I was thinking about moving in with Jennifer, but I knew that was a complete commitment. When I got back, I looked through the paper for apartments. I found a one bedroom not too far away. I called, and the landlord agreed to meet me an hour later. I talked to my mom about my plans, and then went to meet the landlord. The apartment was a subdivision of a large Victorian home. It was beautiful but pretty expensive. I thought about how Nancy could possibly pay for our home and decided I would talk to her about moving back in with her. I thanked the landlord and then drove back to my mother's.

"What did it look like?" my mother asked.

"It's nice, but I can't afford the apartment and my share of the house. I'm going to have to talk Nancy into letting me back in," I said.

"That might be very difficult," she said, "unless you end the affair."

"I'll have to. That's all there is to it," I said.

"It's still going to be difficult," she said.

"I know. I've fucked everything up," I said.

I didn't know if I could give up Jennifer. I thought for a minute that I would get a job teaching again, but I didn't think I could get one. It had been so long since I had taught. I also thought that maybe I could stay with my mother since she lived alone, but I decided against it. I wanted to call Nancy, but I knew she was still angry. I was at a loss.

"Let Nancy cool down. Then you can talk to her," my mother said. "She's a very forgiving person. She might take you back."

"Thanks, Mom, but I don't know," I said.

"It's going to take time," she said.

Chapter 7

A little bit later, I decided to call Nancy again.

"What's up?" she said.

"I've decided never to see Jennifer again, and I can't afford an apartment, so I was thinking of coming back home," I said.

"I'll think about it," she said. "I've got to go now."

She didn't sound as angry as before, but I had to start thinking of breaking it off with Jennifer. I still wanted to be with Jennifer, but thought it was now impossible. I called Jennifer, and she answered right away.

"Hi," she said.

"I've got to talk to you," I said.

"Do you want to come over now? I can get away for an hour," she said.

"Okay," I said.

I told my mother I would be back in a few hours, but I didn't tell her where I was going. I knew I would be tempted by Jennifer, but somehow I would have to resist. I drove over to her place and waited outside. I felt like I was swimming upstream, and the water was cold. She showed up a few minutes later.

"How are you?" she said.

"Not very well," I said.

"Do you want to talk?" she said.

"Yes," I said.

"Sounds serious," she said. "Come on in."

We walked into the apartment, and I watched her as she took of her jacket. Her ass was perfectly round and sticking out. I couldn't resist her.

"Let's talk later," I said.

I kissed her on the eyes, then on the lips. I slowly put my tongue in her mouth and sucked on her lower lip. She responded by sucking on my tongue and putting her hand in my pants. We walked into the bedroom and made love slowly, tenderly. I had never felt such passion. Afterwards, we lay there and stroked each other softly.

"What are you thinking about?" she said.

"You don't want to know," I said.

"Yes, I do," she said.

I have to make a decision, and I can't make one. This morning I thought I should break up with you. Now I'm thinking I should break up with Nancy," I said.

"Well, I like the way you're thinking now. But why do you have to make a decision today? Can't you think about it?" she said.

"I've been thinking about it, but now Nancy knows about you, and I have no place to live," I said.

I told you. You can live with me," she said.

I thought about it for a split second and decided against it. I couldn't give up Nancy, and I couldn't commit to Jennifer at that moment.

"I can't, honey. I love you, but I have a child on the way, and I'm not ready to make a commitment," I said.

"I'll let it go for now, but I'm going to ask again," she said.

"I'd better go," I said.

I put on my clothes, gave her a kiss goodbye, and left. My mind suddenly was in turmoil. I was in the middle of my dilemma, and there was no way out. The passion between Jennifer and me was so intense, I couldn't let it go, but my history with Nancy was too deep to let go also. I went back to my mother's house and made a sandwich. She was out, so I had the place to myself. My mind was spinning. I decided to call Nancy to see how she was feeling.

"What's up?" she said.

"You don't sound as angry as before," I said.

"I've had time to think about it," she said.

"Will you take me back?" I said.

"Not yet," she said.

"Why not?" I said.

"Because I don't trust you," she said.

"I guess I can understand that," I said. "But how long is it going to take before you do trust me?"

"A long time," she said. "You haven't proven anything to me."

"All right. I'll talk to you later," I said.

After I hung up, I was angry with myself. I decided I would have to get a roommate situation that I could afford. I looked through the paper and called four places. The last one sounded good, sharing an apartment with another guy. I called up and made an appointment. When I went to see the place an hour later, I was pleasantly surprised. It was right in the middle of the village, and it was a beautiful apartment. The guy was very friendly. His name was Tony, and we talked for about half an hour. I decided to take the place and left a deposit. I called Nancy and told her I would pick up a few things.

"Where are you going to live?" she said.

"I'm sharing an apartment with another guy," I said.

"Now you can continue your affair," she said.

"I don't want to discuss it. I'll be over in a little while to pick up some clothes," I said.

Now I was angry at Nancy, but I knew it was my anger toward myself that I was turning on her. I drove over to the house and found that Nancy had put two full suitcases of mine on the porch. She obviously didn't want to talk to me, so I left. I went back to my mother's and told her that I had found a place to live. She wasn't happy with me.

"I'm going to move in tonight," I said.

"Why don't you spend the night here and move in tomorrow?" she said.

"I don't know. I feel like settling into my new place," I said.

"Okay by me," she said.

The room was already furnished with a bed and a dresser, so I took my clothes and drove over to my new place. I had a feeling of freedom that I hadn't felt in a long time. I was thinking at that moment in the car, that I could keep seeing Jennifer while trying to keep my marriage alive. I got to the apartment while Tony was watching television and having a beer.

"You want a beer?" Tony said.

"No thanks. I quit drinking," I said.

"I'm watching a movie, but it's almost half over with," he said.

"I'll watch it with you," I said.

I wanted to call Jennifer and tell her about my new

apartment. I walked into my room and called her.

"Hey," she said.

"I got a new place," I said.

"Great! So you're not moving back home?" she said.

"Not now," I said.

"I'll have to check it out," she said. "Can I come over now?"

"Sure. I guess it's all right. My roommate is here," I said.

I gave her the address. It wasn't far away, and she arrived a few minutes later. I introduced her to Tony, and then we went into my room.

"It's a pretty big room," she said.

"Not bad. I need a chair and a nightstand," I said.

"Where are you going to do your painting?" she said.

"I don't know yet. Maybe Tony will let me use a corner of the dining room," I said.

"What did Nancy say the last time you talked to her?" she said.

"She said now that I moved out, I can continue my affair," I said.

"I like that," Jennifer said.

"Well, I don't really know about that. I think I have to separate myself from both of you right now," I said.

"I told you. I'll give you all the space and time you need," she said.

"Good," I said.

She came over to me and kissed me on the cheek. Her kiss was so tender. I kissed her on the mouth, and the next thing you know, we were rolling around on the bed. We made love, and she came twice.

"I thought you needed more time," she said.

"I can't resist you," I said.

"That's good, but maybe it would be better if we took some time off," she said.

"I agree," I said.

We took a shower together. Then she dressed and left. It was getting late, so I went to bed and tried to sleep. I couldn't. I tossed and turned for hours and finally fell asleep about three in the morning. Fortunately, I didn't have to get up early for work, so I slept until nine. When I got up, Tony had already left for work. I made some coffee and decided to call Nancy.

"Hi," she said.

"You don't sound too good," I said.

"I had a horrible night," she said. "I didn't sleep at all."

"I didn't sleep well either," I said.

"What are we going to do?" she said.

"I don't know. I need some time to think," I said.

"Did you sleep with Jennifer last night?" she said.

"No," I said.

"That's all I could think about," she said. "I can't stand the fact that I can't trust you. I always trusted you before."

"I'm sorry," I said.

"That's not good enough," she said.

"What else can I say? I told you I'm not going to see her anymore," I said.

"I don't believe you," she said.

"Don't believe me. I don't care. It's the truth. What more can I say?! I said.

"I'll talk to you later," she said, and hung up.

I was pissed off, but I realized it was mostly at myself for lying to her. I had become a terrible husband, and I wasn't proud of myself. I drank my coffee and got depressed the more I thought about the situation. I knew Nancy was trying to make me feel guilty, and it was working. I felt like I was trudging upstream and kept slipping on the rocks. I ate a bowl of cereal and tried to calm myself down. I wanted to call Jennifer but put it off for a while.

I decided to write some poetry, since I wrote some of my best work when I was upset. I sat at the kitchen table and wrote a poem about fishing in the stream. It was about a man who had a big fish on the line, struggling to bring it in, and finally the fish got away. It turned out better than I expected, but I didn't feel much better after I completed it. I called Greg to see what he was doing. I knew he was working, but I hoped he had a little time to talk to me.

"Hey, what's up?" he said.

"Do you have time to talk?" I said.

"Give me ten minutes. Then I'll call you back," he said.

I waited for a while. Then he called me back.

"What's up, player?" he said.

"Please don't call me that," I said.

"I'm sorry. You don't sound too good," he said.

"I can't make a decision," I said. "I got a place of my own. Nancy won't take me back, and I'm still fooling around with Jennifer."

"Doesn't sound good," he said, "but you don't want to listen to me."

"What should I do?" I said.

"Take a break from both of them, and then beg Nancy to take you back," he said.

"But I can't resist Jennifer," I said.

"There's nothing more I can tell you," he said. "I've got to get back to work. I'll talk to you later."

I felt like I was losing Greg as a friend, but that wasn't foremost in my mind. I had to see Jennifer again. I called her, not knowing what kind of response I would get.

"Hi!" she said.

"Hi yourself," I said.

"I didn't think I would hear from you today," she said.

"I was trying not to call, but I couldn't help myself," I said.

"That's good. I'm so glad you called. What's going on?" she said.

"Not much. I got a poem written," I said.

"About me?" she said.

"Not really, but sort of," I said. "It's a fishing poem?"

"Like the time you saw me naked in the stream?" she said.

"Not exactly," I said.

"Do you want to come over? I can get away for a little while," she said.

"Okay," I said.

I knew I would end up making love to her, no matter what I told myself. Now that I had the freedom of my new place, I felt like I could do whatever I wanted. I still wanted to make up with Nancy, but that would have to wait. I got in the car and found myself driving quickly over to Jennifer's apartment. I made myself slow down, and I started thinking about what I would say to her. She wasn't home yet when I got there, so I waited impatiently for her to arrive. She showed up a little while later.

"Come on in," she said.

I walked in, and for the first time, I found her apartment in disarray.

"Let me pick up quickly," she said.

"You're usually so neat," said.

"You've disrupted my routine," she said.

"I'm sorry," I said.

"Nothing to be sorry about," she said.

After she cleaned up, we sat in the kitchen and had a cup of tea. She looked tired, and I knew I was causing her to lose sleep.

"It's getting colder out," I said. "Winter's coming."

"Yes, but I don't want to talk about the weather," she said. "I want to know what you're thinking."

"I'm confused. I must admit," I said. "I think one thing one minute, the opposite the next."

"Do you want to continue seeing me?" she said.

"Yes, but not every day," I said.

"Every other day? When?" she said.

"I don't know, sweetheart. I can't take all this stress. It's driving me crazy," I said.

"Then let's take a break, like we've been talking about," she said.

"All right. But can we make love one more time?" I said.

"Sure," she said.

We got on top of the bed and kissed, rolling our tongues inside each other's mouths. I knew this was becoming a pattern, but I couldn't resist her. I put my hand under her pants and rubbed her pussy until she got wet. She took my pants off and started sucking on my cock. I got hard right away and flipped her over on the bed, lifting her ass in the air. I wanted to fuck her in the ass, but she wouldn't let me. I penetrated her and fucked her as hard as I could. I was careful not to come inside her, and we fell exhausted on the bed.

"Wow! That was great!" she said. "We should have more problems."

"I have enough problems," I said.

"Listen. Let's really take a break, at least for a few days, so you can clear your mind," she said.

"All right. This time I'll stick to it," I said.

We showered together. Then I dressed and left. I went back to my apartment and sat there thinking. It was as though I was trying to swim upstream, and the fish were all running into me. The water was cold, and I was weary. I was not used to being depressed, but now it was becoming a regular thing. I had lost my sense of humor for the first time in my life, and I didn't know how to regain it. I decided to call Nancy to see how she was feeling.

"Hi," she said.

"What are you doing?" I said.

"Nothing really, trying to write some poetry," she said.

"How's it going?" I said.

"The poetry or me?" she said.

"You," I said.

"I'm not doing well at all. I feel like my whole world had caved in on me," she said. "What about you?"

"I feel the same way," I said.

"What are we going to do about it?" she said. "Are you still sleeping with her?"

"No, I'm not," I said.

"You're lying, Paul. I can tell. I know you. You can't lie to me!" she said.

"I want to come back home. I'll stop seeing her," I said.

"How can I believe you?" she said. "I think you need to stay away for a while and think about the consequences of your actions."

"I miss you. I want to have the baby now. I've thought about it," I said.

"I'll talk to you later," she said, and hung up.

I felt like a jackass and wished now that I had never cheated on her to begin with. My first instinct was to call Jennifer, but I resisted. I had to talk to somebody but didn't think anybody wanted to talk to me. I decided to call Greg, even though I knew he was working.

"What's up, cowboy?" he said.

"I asked Nancy if I could come home, but she won't let me," I said.

"What did you expect? You've got to give her some time," he said. "Did you break it off with Jennifer?"

"Only temporarily," I said.

"That's not going to work either," he said. "I don't know why you don't want to listen to me."

"I've never had better sex in my life. It's got my head turned," I said.

"Well, you'd better get it turned around again," he said. "You're about to lose the best thing in your life. Have you thought about what it might be like for Nancy to raise a child on her own?"

"Yeah, I've thought about it, and it eats me alive," I said.

"You know the sexual attraction between you and Jennifer will wear off, don't you?" he said.

"I know," I said, "but I like her, too. She makes me feel good emotionally."

"I'm done lecturing. You make your own decisions," he said. "I've got to go back to work now."

He was clearly upset, and so was I. He had been my best friend for a long time, and now it seemed like I was losing him. I wanted to call Jennifer in the worst way, but I put it off. I wasn't at home in the apartment and felt very uncomfortable with my free time. I sat down to write but again couldn't concentrate. I had to do something but didn't know what. Finally, I called Jennifer.

"Hi!" she said. "I was hoping to hear from you."

"I know I said that I would stay away for a while, but I'm really lonely," I said.

"I'm lonely too," she said. "I really do love you."

"I love you too," I said. "Do you want to get together and talk?"

"Sure. I'll meet you in half an hour," she said.

I showered and put on some clean clothes. I realized that I felt better when I was planning to see her. I was still somewhat depressed but excited at the same time. I thought about Nancy on the drive over and felt horrible. I wanted to have the passion for Jennifer with Nancy, but it had faded. When I got to Jennifer's place, she was already there.

"Come on in," she said.

"Your place looks a lot neater," I said.

"I'm trying," she said. "Sit down. I'll make a pot of coffee."

I sat down and took a deep breath. I knew I was sinking deeper and deeper into the water.

"Do you want to have children?" I said.

"I think so," she said. "What about you? How are you feeling about Nancy being pregnant?"

"I'm scared to death," I said.

"Maybe you should talk her into having an abortion or giving it up for adoption," she said.

"She wants to keep it," I said.

"That complicates matters, doesn't it?" she said.

"Considerably," I said.

She poured the coffee, and I drank it quickly, thinking it would make me feel better. It didn't. We were all in such a mess. There seemed no way out of it. I thought about having sex with her, but I knew that wouldn't make me feel better either.

"Well, if you're willing to have children with two women, that would be a solution," she said.

"I don't even know if I want to have any children," I said.

"You're having one, it looks like. You'd better get used to it," she said.

"Don't put any more pressure on me," I said.

"I'm sorry. I'm only trying to think of ways to keep you. I don't want to lose you," she said.

"You're not going to lose me, but let's not talk about children anymore," I said.

"All right," she said.

"I have to go," I said. "I'll call you later."

I drove to the grocery store and picked up a few things. Now that I was a bachelor again, I relied on salads and sandwiches. When I got back to the apartment, Tony was there, eating in front of the television. I was miserable. I wanted to go

102

back to the simple life Nancy and I had enjoyed.

"What's up?" Tony said.

"Nothing much," I said.

I went into the kitchen, put the groceries away, and made myself a sandwich. Then I went into my room and sat on the bed, feeling sorry for myself. I decided to go to bed early, but I couldn't fall asleep. I kept thinking about how I had hurt Nancy, and how I still wanted to be with Jennifer. I had no peace. I tried to hypnotize myself to sleep, and finally it worked. I woke up late and found that Tony had already gone to work. I made myself a pot of coffee and thought about calling Jennifer. I also thought about calling Nancy, but I didn't want to hear any lectures. I called Jennifer.

"Hi," she said. "How are you feeling today?"

"I'm still a little depressed, I guess," I said.

"You're starting to make me depressed, too," she said.

"I'm sorry. I don't mean to. Hopefully, it won't last," I said, "but I always feel better talking to you."

"That's good. Do you want to get together today?" she said.

"Sure. What time?" I said.

"Come over now. I don't have an appointment for a few hours," she said.

I took a shower quickly and put on some clothes. I was excited to see her, but I had a nagging feeling about Nancy. I drove to Jennifer's place, and all I could think about was Nancy. When I got there, Jennifer had some coffee and toasted me a bagel.

"Have you thought about marrying me?" she said.

"I thought you weren't going to put more pressure on me,"

I said.

"I won't. I'm sorry," she said, "but I have to think about my future, too."

"We have plenty of time. You're still very young," I said.

"Did you talk to Nancy today?" she asked.

"No. I'm afraid of what she'll say, but I'll have to call her later," I said.

"I bet she's very angry," Jennifer said.

"That's putting it mildly," I said.

"Are you more in love with me that you are with her?" she said.

"Yes," I said.

"Then there's no debate," she said.

"But I still feel guilty," I said.

"You're going to have to get over her. Sometimes love hurts," she said.

"I don't know if I can get over her," I said.

"You have to choose," she said.

"I know," I said.

"Well, I'm not in the mood to make love. Is there anything else you want to say?" she said.

"No. It's time for me to go. I can see that," I said.

I left, and now I knew they were both mad at me. I drove home in a state of depression and sulked when I got to the apartment. I decided to call Nancy, hoping desperately that she would make me feel better.

"Hi," she said.

"Hi," I said.

"What's up?" she said.

"I feel horrible," I said.

"So do I," she said.

"Can't we get back together?" I said.

"I'm thinking about it," she said.

"Are you really?" I said.

"Yes, even though I know you're still seeing Jennifer," she said.

"I'll break up with her. I promise. I just want the life we had before," I said.

"I do too. I'm so lonely, but I still don't trust you," she said.

"I'll earn your trust. I promise that too. I'll behave myself. I just got scared. That's all," I said.

"I'll think about it," she said.

"That's all I ask," I said.

"Goodbye," she said.

"Bye," I said.

She made me feel so much better. Now it was up to me to break it off with Jennifer I decided to call Jennifer right away and break off the relationship on the phone.

"What's up?" she said.

"I have to talk to you," I said.

"Sounds serious," she said.

"It is," I said.

"Here we go," she said.

"I have to break up with you. I've made a new commitment to Nancy, and that's all there is to it," I said.

"That's fine. Call me if you change your mind. No, I take that back. Don't call me anymore," she said, and hung up.

I felt like a large burden had been lifted off my shoulders. I called Nancy right back.

"Hi," she said, laughing.

"I broke up with her," I said.

"Good," she said. "Now pack up your things and come home."

"Okay," I said.

In three hours, I had all my things back at the house. I could actually fell my sense of humor returning. Nancy and I sat down for a cup of coffee.

"I'm going to watch you like a hawk," she said.

"That's fine with me," I said.

"How did she take it?" she said.

"Not very well, but she didn't scream," I said.

"I still love you," she said.

After a while, I rebuilt my trust with Nancy. We had the baby, and now the three of us are a happy little family.